D1741305

Marc Antony Cutler is a 40 year old writer from Stanford Le Hope in Essex. He currently lives in Hull with his wife Hayley and boisterous border collie Bruce. He has written 3 novels, various short stories and a collection of poetry.

If you'd like to contact Marc you can email him at:
smalltownstranger@gmail.com

Withdrawn from Suffolk Libraries

This book is dedicated to my grandparents:
Peter Cutler, Muriel Cutler,
Albert John Harman, and Mabel Harman.

Prologue

The shadowy figure blended perfectly into the darkness, crouched low on the wet sand. Dressed head to toe in black, they watched the house in the distance with the ease of binoculars.

The sound of the waves lapped rhythmically behind as the figure intruded on the unaware family's evening.

This was the best part: the watching, the waiting, and the knowing what was to come. To see their smiles and to witness their joy. Unaware their lives could and would be torn apart, their happy carefree existence forever altered.

To have that power and control was exhilarating.

The figure in the night breathed heavily, excitement building. It was almost time.

Chapter One

James Bradfield stared out over the sea as the sun set on the Edgartown Lighthouse. He'd grown up in Martha's Vineyard, or 'The Yard' as he liked to call it. Despite that, he knew he would never tire of the sight of the sun setting over the lighthouse.

James was startled from his whimsical daydream by the sound of the vacuum cleaner roaring into life behind him. He turned around to see his wife, Claire, giving the vacuum one hell of a task. The floor was a mess, with bits of paper, bits of food, and nice large chunks of chocolate cake walked soundly into the carpet as if a parade of soldiers had recently been through the house.

James looked back at the tip of the sun slowly disappearing behind the lighthouse and then back at the bombsite that was his living room. Contrasting views if ever he'd seen them.

The house wasn't normally this untidy, of course; in fact, it was usually immaculately clean. Too tidy, some might say. Today, however, was the exception, because today was his son Jake's eighth birthday party.

For a while, Claire had been displaying signature marks of an Obsessive-Compulsive Disorder. James had first noticed it about a year following Jake's birth. Everything had to be in its right place, facing the right way in all the cupboards and on all the surfaces and all the time. Mess and disarray was not allowed. Sometimes, in fact often when you have a small child, it is unavoidable.

The party had been James' idea and as the house became more unruly throughout the day, he sensed Claire becoming more on edge. No sooner had the last child dispersed than she kicked into cleaning action. Claire had been chomping at the bit for hours.

It had been quite a day. Most of the kids from the school came and the majority of them had a good day. They had all consumed too much fizzy drink, excesses of sugary food and probably too much fun, if there was such a thing. James was uncertain that any of those children would be sleeping early tonight.

Thanks to the largely uninterrupted summer weather they had in Edgartown, planning a party was always a fairly reliably staged event.

Jake had been in his element. His friends from school were there and he'd received a sackload of gifts, and a few doubles as well. They'd sort that out later though. James had a giant bouncy castle erected. It was in the shape of a basketball court and had nets inside it as well; all the kids loved it. He'd also gotten a local clown in. Not to say the guy was a clown so to speak, but he performed as the circus variety. That particular idea had received a disappointingly lackluster response from the children. Some of the kids loved it, some of the kids were petrified. The clown had been kind of scary, practically miserable; he even had a down turned mouth painted on. Still, some of the kids found his water-filled flower hilarious and he made some interesting shapes out of the balloons for them. All in all, the day had been a success.

James turned and bypassed the vacuum, pecked Claire on the cheek, and made his way up the wooden spiral staircase to Jake's bedroom. Jake was zonked out on his bed already, clothes still on, one foot hanging off the bed. *Put another twelve years on him,* James thought, *and he'll be striking that same pose, only because of something a little stronger than cake!* James thought about waking Jake up. He wasn't sure if Jake had cleaned his teeth or not. He'd eaten a lot of sugary food today and the last thing James wanted was for Jake to end up with cavities. He went into the bathroom and picked Jake's Transformers toothbrush up out of the pot that the family brushes sat in. The bristles were wet. Of course, that could have been from this morning's clean, but it was enough to convince James to leave Jake alone. As with most people, Jake wasn't the happiest if he was woken up before his time. James went back into the bedroom and tucked Jake under the covers. He could leave the T-shirt and shorts he was wearing on for now. They'd be his pajamas tonight. Despite the fact that the weather rarely broke 90 degrees in Edgartown, it tended to get a little cool at night, mainly due to the breeze blowing in off the sea.

James went over to close Jake's curtains and had a look out at the dusky scenery. Lapping waves, literally twenty feet away, meekly dashed against the shore. The stars were bright tonight; it would be a cold one overnight. He looked over at Memorial Bridge, which sat across Sengekontacket pond where Jake loved to play. Perfect scenery for a perfect day.

James kissed Jake on the forehead and made his way back down the stairs, where, to his delight, Claire had finished tidying up. If anyone visited now they would never have known a party had taken place. Of course, if anyone visited now, they would be turned away. Neither Claire nor James were fans of impromptu uninvited guests. They both found that particular behavior quite rude and intrusive, especially late in the evening. There was a globally accepted unwritten cut-off time.

Claire was standing in the dining room reading a magazine over the table.

James approached her from behind, wrapped his hands around her waist, and kissed her on the neck.

'Went well today, babe, didn't it?' he said, as a matter of fact rather than a question. She maneuvered herself from his grasp and span round to face him, his arms still around her.

'Yeah, they loved it but I am shattered now!' she kissed him on the lips. 'We should have done this yesterday; you have to go to work tomorrow.'

'I know,' James answered, 'but his birthday is today. It's been a long day but the look on his face, more than once as well, was priceless.'

Claire smiled. She knew exactly what James meant. Kids tend to get excited, go a little mad with excitement even, and Jake had been like that from the moment he pulled back the covers and his feet hit the carpet that morning. He was a happy kid at the best of times but today he was literally overjoyed. For her, that was a joy to behold. Claire hadn't had much of a childhood herself so the opportunity to live that through her own child was magnificently priceless.

Claire's parents had divorced while she was still a toddler. It was a result of her mother's drinking and cheating, not her father, as is often the scenario. She had stayed with her mum, her dad leaving never to be seen again.

5

As Claire was two years old at the time, she had only vague, fuzzy recollections of him. Anything she learned about him came via the mouth of Sheila, her mother's sister. After years of watching her mother's alcohol abuse and a catalogue of supposed stepdads, many of whom abused her physically and emotionally, Claire made a decision. At fifteen she went to live with Sheila, and remained there until she eventually met James.

Claire still spoke to her mother via telephone but the conversations were rare and always terse and tense. James often marveled at how Claire's character changed completely during those brief interludes.

James and Claire walked over to the patio doors and stepped out onto the white decking. The moonlight was now bouncing off the sea in random wispy shapes, like a patch of spilt milk in the ocean.

'I take it the birthday boy has gone to sleep already?' James asked rhetorically. Claire nodded her head silently.

A shooting star burst across the night sky as if it were a lone firework escaping from the stockpile awaiting the July 4th parade.

Claire wrapped her arm around James' waist and looked out in front of her. Standing there with the four-bedroom house behind her and their son asleep upstairs, there was little more perfect than any of this. James was a hard worker, a financial accountant for a firm in town, and she'd been lucky to meet him. There was a lot of truth to be had in the belief of fate.

The two of them had met at a conference in Massachusetts ten years previously and had hit it off straight away.

Claire was a legal secretary at the time. James had made her laugh the moment they first spoke; his humor was near the knuckle, to say the least, and she liked that about him. She liked that he didn't care what anybody thought about him. He was who he was, take it or leave it. They had a common interest in film and music. The one main similarity, however, was their desire to find 'the one', get married, settle down, and have children. Claire hadn't met a guy who genuinely wanted to have kids before. Having children was all she wanted; she wasn't career-minded and she knew she would be a good mum, mainly because hers hadn't been. For many years she had had no time for her own mum, because she had been such a terrible influence on her life growing up. Now, however, she realized she had a lot to thank her for, because without her own upbringing Claire wouldn't have known just how easily she could do it the right way.

James and Claire had been married less than a year later and Jake had been born just over a year after that. Unfortunately, due to some complications, the chances of having any more children were taken away from them. She had been mortified at the time, as had James, but the two of them knew that, as with everything, it all happens for a reason. They dedicated their life to making Jake's life as much fun and as happy as they could, and thus far had succeeded in spades.

James broke her recollecting thought. 'It's perfect out here,' he said. Claire couldn't have agreed more.

The following day came and went as they often do. Work was busy for James but that was a given at the start of each day. He liked being busy though because ultimately, the busier he was the quicker the day went. He worked close to home, about a five-minute drive; however, it was a half-hour walk if he ever felt like it. He often did walk it but today the sky had been overcast and although little rain fell in Edgartown, when it did fall, it was torrential. The last thing James wanted was to turn up at the office looking like a wet T-shirt competitor.

James arrived home at about a quarter to six and the sun was still shining overhead, glimmering on the sea like a bed of mirrors. He'd decided on the way home to start a BBQ on the beach. The evening had turned out much nicer than the day had predicted and he figured Claire wouldn't have started dinner yet. James pulled his station wagon up outside and made his way into the house. It was unusually quiet. 'Claire, Jake?' he called out, but there was no answer. He looked out into the yard but neither of them were out there either. He figured Claire had taken Jake into town, which wasn't unusual. He momentarily thought about texting his wife but, having almost a phobia of texting, decided against it. He'd hold off starting the BBQ though in case Claire had taken Jake for tea in town. She had done that before as well, although it did mildly annoy him because he'd just come from town himself, so could have joined them. Still, it gave James the opportunity to throw on an LP and listen to some music. He was a sucker for a record. Despite being in his early thirties, James wasn't about to adapt to the MP3 lifestyle. He'd still not quite gotten his head around the Compact Disc; he just loved a record. He took an immaculate copy of Fleetwood Mac's 'Rumours' out of its sleeve and placed it on the turntable. He loved everything about records. The way they shined, the way the speakers crackled with electricity as the arm was brought down and the needle connected, as if bringing the whole stereo to life.

The opening chords of 'Second Hand News' blasted from the speakers, bringing James whole house to life with sound. Christine McVie's vocals kicked in and the whole album came alive pumping through the house to James' joy.

Walking over to the dining room and opening the fridge, James thought about cracking open a cold beer. A cold beer, however, just didn't seem to fit his mood. He made his way to the wine rack. Now a glass of red, that was the missing piece in this relaxation jigsaw. He settled on a bottle of Californian Cabernet Sauvignon and poured himself a generous helping into the largest wine glass in the cupboard. They had a set of six wine glasses and for some reason, unknown to either Claire or himself, a much larger glass on its own. It was shaped like a wine glass; it wasn't a brandy glass, as one of their visitors had suggested. *What the hell*, James thought anyway. Today it was a wine glass. James cut a small piece of cheese off the block in the fridge, to savor with the wine. He was now quite enjoying his alone time. It had been a generally shitty day at work if he thought about it, which he wasn't about to do. He sat down in the comfy leather armchair to enjoy the wine, cheese, and sounds of Seventies progressive rock. He was aware that in his head he was somehow trying to justify the reasons why he was enjoying the alone time, as if he should feel guilty. He had a habit of doing that. He did so much for his family, which he in no way begrudged, that when it came to doing something specifically for him he felt as if he was doing his family some kind of injustice. The album was in full swing now as Stevie Nick's rasping tones sang about love gone bad in 'Dreams'. It was one of his favorite songs on the album, one of his favorite songs of all time. Typically, it was about to be interrupted. The sound of the phone ringing startled him out of his tranquil music-and-wine abyss. James thought about ignoring it but then figured it could be Claire. He turned the music down slightly and answered the phone with 'Hello?', instantly annoyed to hear a male voice.

'Is that a Mr. James Bradfield?' the man on the other end asked.

'Yes, it is. How can I help you?' James answered cordially, one ear tuned to 'Never Going Back' as it played quietly in the background.

'I have a question for you, Mr. Bradfield,' the voice on the other end interrupted.

'Who is this?' James asked.

'I have a question for you,' the man said again, in practically the same tone.

'Who am I talking to?' James asked in an exasperated tone, becoming slightly agitated by the man on the other end's evasiveness.

'Do you love your wife and child, Mr. Bradfield?' the voice on the other end asked. The sounds of the music were instantly shut out of James' head.

'What did you say?' James asked, knowing full well what he had heard but hoping that he had been mistaken.

'I asked you if you love your wife and child, Mr. Bradfield?'

'Of course I do,' James shouted down the phone. 'Where are they? What have you done to them?' he screamed.

'Calm down, Mr. Bradfield, I have done absolutely nothing to them. They are perfectly fine. Whether it remains that way is entirely up to you.' The man sounded as though he was smiling, laughing even. He was enjoying this. James felt enraged, confused, and physically sick all at the same time.

'Please, whoever you are, whatever you want, I will give it to you,' James said, beginning now to plead to the faceless voice on the phone.

'Money, Mr. Bradfield? You think I want money, don't you?' the man responded calmly. 'No, no, Mr. Bradfield, it is much simpler than that. I merely want a decision from you. You can make a decision, can't you?' The man asked in a condescending way.

James thought for a moment and began to get angry with himself. In a matter of moments he had believed everything the man on the other end had said. Did this man have Claire and Jake? What really was going on here? James tried to think logically.

'I don't know who you are,' he said calmly and steadily, 'I don't know if you are telling the truth. If you have my son and my wife, let them go or I am hanging up and calling the police.' James thought the logicalness of his statement would solve the problem.

'By all means call the police, Mr. Bradfield. I enjoy the chase, really I do,' the man on the other end replied. 'You have 72 hours to make your decision, Mr. Bradfield.'

'What decision? You haven't asked me to make any decision,' James replied, the panic in his voice starting to rise again.

'Which one lives and which one dies,' the man answered, in his cool, calculated tone.

Everything around James seemed to stop. Time stood still. He could hear his heart beating, his pulse throbbing. The remnants of the mouthful of wine sat on his tongue in a foul vinegar film.

'I can't make that decision; nobody could make that decision! You're insane!' James screamed. 'Let them go!'

'72 hours, Mr. Bradfield. Which one do you love more?' the voice said. 'Decide and one will be set free. Fail to decide and they will both die. Either way, Mr. Bradfield, you have a life-changing decision to make for someone.' The line went dead as the man on the other end hung up. James stared at the blank magnolia wall in front of him as he let the handset slip to the floor, bashing itself on the table leg as it fell.

The sounds of Lindsey Buckingham beating out the words 'Don't stop thinking about tomorrow,' echoed around the house, but James Bradfield didn't hear them.

Chapter Two

Chief Inspector Anthony Leith sat in his oak rocking chair, slowly tipping himself backwards and forwards. He looked out of the window at the sea lapping the shore but felt nothing more than innate boredom. He was one of two officers in the Edgartown Force. His young deputy, Jennifer Clearwater, had already left for home. He looked at the watch his wife, Clarice, had bought him and observed the second hand tick away.

Nothing ever really happened in Edgartown, which was great for the islanders but not so for him. His job was by and large taken up by mostly irrelevant townsfolk squabbles which invariably could have been sorted out without his intervention in the first place.

Anthony had originally intended to become a police officer in Massachusetts. However, life had transpired against him and he found himself stuck in Edgartown twenty-five years on. Now, at the age of forty-five, he was resigned to the fact that life would be played out here. As he watched a small fishing boat chugging its way back to shore he realized his ship had long since sailed.

Despite the fact that nothing ever happened, he was a stickler for the rules. There was still five minutes left on his shift and the people of Edgartown paid his salary. He never had clocked off early and he never would. If there were any troubles after hours the whole town had his personal number. That was what living in a small community meant. It meant that he was always there for them if they needed him. In twenty-five years his number had been called out of hours just three times.

The first was a wrong number, so it didn't count, but it had been called. The second time was from Old Man Whelks, and that had been a heart-wrenching call. His wife, Mabel, had passed away and George Whelks had found her. She'd gone peacefully enough, in her sleep, but he didn't know what to do. He called Anthony that night because he had no idea who else to call. It was a sad night and a sad time and Anthony spent that evening and many subsequent evenings sitting with George Whelks. It wasn't long afterwards that he passed as well. Although Anthony felt that if there were such a thing as the afterlife, then Mr. Whelks would certainly be happier spending it with his Mabel.

The final time his phone had startled him after hours was due to a small prank in town between Matt Reedler and Frankie Jenkins. Both had been drinking too much and both ran into each other. Kind of standard stuff, and Anthony had chucked them in the cells for the night to sleep it off. There were no casualties or injuries apart from those suffered by the boys' egos, and he let them go without charge the following morning. There were three cells in Edgartown's Police Department. Three cells and two police officers. It figured really; there were too many of both. That, of course, was another thing about living in a small community. It seemed as though everybody knew each other and invariably nobody really wanted to see anybody charged with a crime. Outwardly, they all perceived themselves to be friends.

Anthony had always wanted to be in charge of keeping the peace. When the peace kept itself without much help being necessary, he felt fairly redundant most of the time.

To most people, it was the ideal job. Sitting around doing nothing most days, or out on the street in gorgeous weather with glorious views. Your life never really being in any danger, everybody knowing you by first name, and everybody appearing to like you. For Anthony, though, it felt like a life wasted all the same. He'd grown up watching the likes of Starsky & Hutch and Hawaii Five-O and he wanted the excitement and fun programs like that depicted. As he got older he watched shows like Hill Street Blues and wanted the grimy, gritty side of police work. It never came.

Still, there were worse things, he guessed, he just didn't want to be forty-five and wonder where his life had gone. He loved his wife, Clarice, with all his heart. They were the same age, had met at school and never been apart. They couldn't have kids but he'd never really wanted any; he figured he wouldn't be good at it. Clarice never really seemed interested either. Anthony had always figured that if they really wanted children then they would adopt. Neither of them

12

had ever expressed an interest in adopting and the subject was never broached. Now, though, he couldn't help but wonder if that was what his life had always been missing. Both he and Clarice had recently discussed the way he'd been feeling but she continuously put his disheartenment and wavering moods down to a mid-life crisis. This depressed him even more. Not so much the possibility Clarice may be right, but the thought that he could have another forty-five years of this to go.

Anthony switched off his computer and the desk lamp and rose from the rocking chair ready to make his way home. Then, the telephone rang. Anthony immediately figured it would be Clarice. If the phone rang twenty times a day then nineteen of those would be his wife. However when he lifted the receiver all he could hear was a man, sobbing uncontrollably.

'Hello, who is this?' Anthony asked, disturbed by the distress on the other end of the phone. 'Listen, calm down whoever this is and tell me what the problem is' he followed up with.

The man on the other end of the phone started to compose himself.

'It's James Bradfield, my wife, my wife and my son, they're gone, they've been taken,' James said breathlessly.

Anthony stopped for a second. What James was telling him was illogical and sounded unlikely as well, in this town at least.

'Are you sure they've been taken?' Anthony asked. There was a long pause before James answered the question.

'They've been taken by a fucking maniac, Anthony. You need to get over here.'

Anthony didn't even offer a response, he threw the phone down on the receiver and ran out to his car. He hoped to God this was some kind of awful and elaborate practical joke, but he'd known James Bradfield for a long time and he just wasn't the type to pull such a stunt, especially at the expense of his family who he adored. It seemed ironic that after years of waiting, practically willing something awful to happen to make his job worthwhile, Anthony was now hoping that what he'd just heard was nothing more than some drink-fuelled hoax.

A quarter of an hour later Anthony arrived at the Bradfield residence. All of the lights were on. He knocked on the crisply painted front door and it opened immediately, as if James had been sitting there waiting for

13

him to arrive. He didn't say anything, just walked off into the lounge and slumped in the arm chair, with Anthony following close behind him. The room was silent with the exception of the record which had long since come to an end, still revolving with the needle skipping endlessly over and over against the edge of the label. Anthony walked over and lifted the arm and put it back in its cradle before sitting in the chair opposite James.

It had been a long time since Anthony had seen a vinyl record. He approved of Bradfield's choice and then instantly realized that James would never be able to listen to Fleetwood Macs 'Rumours' in the same way again. Music always resonates throughout the good and the bad and becomes affixed to that memory forever more.

For the next twenty minutes Anthony listened and took notes as James relayed the story to him, culminating with its chilling conclusion.

Anthony was shocked but at the same time logical. What had happened to James was awful but there was nothing to suggest it was going to culminate in whoever had made that call carrying out their threats.

'Listen James we all know each other in this town, even if it's only to nod a daily hello to, and I cannot see anybody carrying this out. I just can't,' Anthony said.

James looked at him intensely 'If it were you're family, would you be saying that? You'd be sitting there feeling like I am, fearing the worst,' James said. 'What do I do?'

Anthony thought for a moment. He genuinely didn't know, they had nothing to go on.

'Your wife, she drives don't she? I didn't see her car out there,' Anthony said.

'Yeah she drives but it's usually in the garage, though I figured she'd taken it into town. Well, before that phone call anyway. I haven't checked,' James answered.

'Well, first and foremost let's see if her car is still here, because whether it is or it isn't may offer some clues,' Anthony said.

They went around to the garage and James opened the door. There was the blue Ford Coupe sitting there where it usually was.

'So she was taken from home then,' James said, looking at the car.

'Or went willingly,' Anthony responded.

James looked puzzled. 'Why would she go willingly?' he asked.

Anthony tried to think of the best way to direct his response to that question but decided bluntness was probably the key.

'How have you and your wife been getting on lately? Do you think there is a possibility she's left with someone else and he's playing you for a fool?' Anthony asked the question, instantly annoyed with himself for doing so, judging by the look on James face.

'That's a fucking ludicrous suggestion. My wife and I are fine, and we always have been. That's… that's…nonsensical,' he finished.

Anthony figured he was probably right, but deep down he was looking for a more logical, less frightening conclusion, because if what James was telling him about the call was true, then they could be embarking on a serious problem. The other alternative and the one that Anthony found himself leaning to was equally as awful. What if James Bradfield had murdered his family and was now using some elaborate story as an opportunity for an alibi? That possibility stuck in his throat like an overcooked steak but he had to consider it.

'We have no leads at present, there's nothing to go on,' Anthony retreated. 'Try and get some rest and I'll call Eric Blane over at the Oak Bluffs PD in the morning and see if he can spare a couple of men to help out.'

'How the hell do you expect me to rest when my family are missing? They're with some maniac who could be doing God knows what to them,' James said, before breaking down again.

Anthony put his arm around James' shoulder. 'Listen, one thing he said to you was that they would come to no harm until you have made your decision. We have time to find him and we will.' Anthony hoped he sounded more convincing than he felt. If this was really happening then it was out of his remit and out of the town's depth.

He got back in his car and started out home. He'd call Eric Blane at Oak Bluffs first thing - he was sure he'd be able to spare some men. Oak Bluffs was a small town just North of Edgartown but it had its own police force with a few extra hands. Eric was a good guy and Anthony knew that once he relayed this story to him he'd be only too happy to throw his hat in the ring. Oak Bluffs had a lot in common with Edgartown. It too had a zero crime rate.

Chapter Three

Eric Blane sat at the large wooden breakfast table in his dining room practically inhaling his fourth golden syrup covered pancake. Eric was a short, large man whose girth was not assisted by his wife, Mildred. She insisted on making every meal contain at least twice the recommended daily dose of saturated fat. Some may say Mildred's incessant need to fill Eric's arteries with more cholesterol than a fast food chain was tantamount to manslaughter. Everybody, except Eric it would seem, was aware he would not be making it to a ripe old age. In fact Mildred's love of her husband made her blind to the damage she was doing. She just wanted to make him happy. Food made him happy, ecstatic even. Most people who knew Eric were surprised he was 45. Nobody that obese should live that long, it would seem.

As pancake number five made its way into Eric's slobbering, toothy cavern, his mobile phone lit up. His ring tone was the standard ringing of many a phone. It would have been no surprise had it been Weird Al Yankovic's Michael Jackson pastiche, 'Eat It.'

Through a mouth still full of food Eric managed a single, two syllable word 'hello' before proceeding to sit, listen and nod his head at nobody in particular occasionally between mouthful's of gluttonous food. Despite what he was being told on the other end of the phone his appetite wasn't about to diminish. He finished the call and his contribution to the conversation with the words 'Be there soon' and hung up.

'Who was that?' his wife asked, as she fired up the frying pan for yet more pancakes.

'Tony Leith, over at Edgartown, wants me to take one of the boys down there they have a problem,' Eric answered.

'Oh, right I see,' Mildred responded 'I take it you won't be wanting these pancakes then.'

'Nah always room for more pancakes and if I know old Tony it's probably a drama being made out of a crisis. You know what that Edgartown lot is like,' he said, salivating at the prospect of another helping of breakfast. Just then a Third World appeal appeared on his TV screen. 'Turn that off Mildred,' he said. 'It puts me off my food.' On Eric's behalf, no irony had been intended.

Eric Blane's Police Vehicle rolled up outside the Edgartown Police Department and he rolled out, the car visibly lifting as he did. His passenger, Officer Jed Dooley climbed out the other side. Jed was over six feet tall and as skinny as a rake. He contrasted Blane in every physical aspect. Eric took his time to get round the other side of the car and made his way up the steps to the entrance. Jed had shot up them with ease and watching the chief climb them himself took more effort.

'You OK there Chief?' Jed asked him. This question being asked more regularly as the weeks went on it would seem. Eric as usual failed to answer. He gave Jed a knowing glance though as if to say 'what the hell has it got to do with you?'. Jed's concern was genuine at least. He had a lot of time for the chief and he really dreaded the day something would happen to him. Like everybody else he felt that day was approaching by the second.

The two men made their way into the small cramped room that housed both of Edgartown's Police Department and Deputy Jennifer Clearwater greeted both the men. Jed had a thing for her, he always had. Jenny was in her early thirties and him his late twenties. Both of them were single and they'd been out a couple of times in the past and got on well but it was never any more than that. The last time the two of them had been out was for a Jaws fest at the Edgartown cinema. They'd watched the first Jaws film in the theatre because it was on to celebrate the anniversary of the film. He'd taken her over to the steakhouse opposite and they'd had a good laugh at the blanket you could clearly see under Robert Shaw's back as the shark bit through him. He'd wondered how he had never spotted that before, he'd seen that film a dozen times. As they were about to go their separate ways Jed had leaned in for a kiss, and Jenny had leaned back. It was awkward, uncomfortably so and the two of them said their goodbyes and away they went. That was six months ago and they hadn't spoken since, not even by text message.

Jenny stood there in her Edgartown Police uniform her red hair flowing over her shoulders and resting on the front, just above her breasts. Her green eyes seemed to perpetually twinkle like emerald stars emanating from her features.

She smiled at Jed but through the smile the awkwardness still shone.

Chief Leith walked in. Everybody was very informal when it came to addressing each other. Nobody went by titles in the local police forces; they all knew each other too well. To the townsfolk he was the chief but to Jed and Eric, he was Tony.

'Hi Tony, been a while,' Eric said, extending his hand as a welcome. The chief took his clammy hand and shook it firmly.

'It's nice to see you Eric, just wish it was under better circumstances,' Anthony replied. He nodded in the direction of Jed 'How you doing Jed?' He nodded in reply and shrugged his shoulders indicating he was feeling 'so so' at best.

'We have to assume this guy is being serious,' Anthony suddenly said making it clear the pleasantries were now out of the way. 'Mrs. Bradfield and her son Jake are officially missing,' he continued.

'Where were they last seen?' Eric asked.

Anthony began to answer but Jenny interrupted. 'I called the school as soon as it opened this morning to make them aware Jake wouldn't be in as there had been a situation. From what we can gather Claire Bradfield collected her son from school and went home. Their whereabouts after that is unclear,' she said.

'How do we know they went home?' Jed enquired.

'The car is in the garage,' Tony answered. 'She always picks Jake up by car because it's too far to walk.'

'Kids these days,' Eric said. 'They're spoilt, can't take a bit of exercise.'

Jenny, Tony and Jed all seemed to look at each other at the same time, raising their eyebrows in unison. If there was one thing Eric was totally oblivious too, other than his obvious poor health, it was irony.

'I suggest we all make our way round town and speak to as many people as we can and find out if anybody saw anything suspicious yesterday between the times of 4pm and 6pm,' Tony said.

'Why those times specifically though?' Jed asked.

'Because we know Claire picked Jake up from school at 3.30pm and we know they got home again,' Jenny answered. 'We have to assume they were taken between 4pm and 6pm when Mr. Bradfield took the call.'

'Yeah, Mr. Bradfield,' Eric said. 'Anyone considered this guy may be behind this?'

'It crossed my mind Eric, but no,' Tony replied 'James is a good guy. I've known him a long time, he wouldn't do that. I just can't see it.'

Eric pondered this for a while, his hand thumbing his chin. 'OK, but why don't I question him anyway?' he said 'As you say, you've known him a long time, maybe your opinion is a bit biased when it comes to this guy.'

'I'm not averse to you questioning him,' Anthony said, clearly put out by the suggestion he could be unprofessional. 'Give it a go. Like you say, you never know.'

'I'll go over there straight away,' Eric said. 'I know where the place is I think.'

'How'd you know, you ever been there before?' Jed asked.

'Kind of, yeah,' Eric answered. 'There's a lovely fresh fish stall down there.' He was right, of course, there was.

'Jed and I will go around town and see if we can find anything out,' Anthony said. 'Jenny, why don't you go to the school and speak to the teachers and see if you can get details of the parents, give them a call as well,' he finished.

Jenny nodded her head in the affirmative. The four police officers made their way outside, three of them much quicker than the other.

Terrence Denton looked at himself in the mirror. He needed a shave and he looked like he hadn't slept for days. He hadn't. He was a reasonably good looking man. Tall, well built, deep set brown eyes and cropped black hair. He bared his teeth at the mirror they were slightly black. Not blackened by decay however but stained from the bottle of red he'd enjoyed the night before. The wine however hadn't helped him sleep at all, as alcohol used to. Even if he did doze off for a while he knew he'd be plagued by the nightmares again. For so long now, the nightmares invaded his sleep. He couldn't remember what it was like to just have a normal dream. Everything was so sick, twisted and violent, always so very violent and so very real.

He cleaned his teeth until the only discoloration in the toothpaste foam was that of his bleeding gums. His teeth were now their natural off color white. He didn't think anybody outside of the movies or television actually had those fluorescent white teeth anyway.

As he looked at his reflection an old lady with long straggled grey hair appeared in the doorway behind him. He turned and walked out of the bathroom, past the aged woman, without saying a word. He walked the long oak paneled corridor of his house, completely ignoring the suave silver haired gentleman standing near the top of the stairs and down them he trotted. Walking into the brightly lit kitchen swathed in sunlight, he paid no attention to the young woman leaning over the sink, her back to him. She turned to face him, and most of her features were missing. Half of her face was open, showing the jaw and tongue in all its bloody glory and her hair was matted with blood where most of the skull was also missing, her brain in full view, glistening in its thin membrane. Her left eye hung out of its socket and hung on what had once been a cheek.

Terrence looked at her and jumped slightly, indeed much less than anyone who'd initially viewed such a sight would.

'Thank-you Veronica' he said 'you can put that away now' the woman bowed her head and when she raised it again her face was completely normal. She was quite a beautiful woman in fact.

Since the age of eleven Terrence had been able to see those who had passed on. He'd been hit by a car on the corner of his road and suffered some considerable head trauma. His Doctors and parents had not expected him to survive. The surgeon had told his mum and dad that even if he did live he would be likely to spend the rest of his life in a wheelchair, trapped in a vegetative state.

Terrence had defied all odds, not only re-emerging from his comatose state but also making a full recovery. At least, that was how it seemed at the beginning but as time moved on he became acutely aware that things had changed.

His first real recollection was of a young boy he befriended in his bedroom by the name of Davy Merrison. To everybody else Terrence had adopted some kind of imaginary friend. His parents feared he was too old for such a thing and Denton's constant argument that Davy was real concerned them greatly. However given the shock and trauma of the accident just six months previously, they let it slide convincing themselves it was a coping mechanism.

The following Christmas Terrence was playing in his room with the boy nobody could see as he had been the previous 4 months. Davy began to tell Terrence a story about how he'd been trapped in a car with his parents and died in a fire. His relay of events culminated in Davy showing Terrence just what being trapped in that car had done to him.

Terrence would never forget what he saw that day just as his parents would never forget his screams. He never did see Davy Merrison again, only when he closed his eyes.

After many months and years of visiting psychiatrists and various Doctors he was eventually seen by someone who, quite rightly, decided that what Terrence had was indeed a gift and not an affliction at all.

Now as a twenty seven year old man Terrence Denton was considered one of the foremost Psychic Mediums in Massachusetts. Whilst he still faced daily ridicule from the press and public he was generally well respected and highly regarded. He had solved many missing persons cases and although the majority of them ended in heartbreak for somebody he had given closure to many.

'You don't have to do that Veronica, I know what happened to you here,' he continued, talking to the apparition at the sink. 'We can share this house, we've discussed this already' he finished, sternly. The woman skulked off out of the kitchen, her head hanging low, looking downbeat and defeated.

Terrence smiled to himself at the thought of anybody else witnessing him telling the kitchen sink off.

Chapter Four

Eric Blane made his way up the front steps of the Bradfield residence. The place was well looked after, these were clearly people who took pride in their property, that was obvious.

James Bradfield opened the door before Eric had time to knock.

'Can I help you?' he asked. Eric didn't know James Bradfield, had probably never even seen him before. What he did know from looking at him, was this man hadn't slept. His eyes were glassy and the bags under them were so big they'd need clearance at an airport. That wasn't just from not sleeping though, he'd clearly been crying.

To Eric there was one of two reasons for this. The obvious being that Bradfield was in a terrible state over the disappearance of his family. Indeed who wouldn't be, but there was always the possibility of a flip side. Eric also wondered if this man's appearance was as a result of stress induced from killing his family himself. Whilst little ever happened in Martha's Vineyard Eric read enough of the press and watched more than enough television to know that the world was full to the brim with crazy people.

He reached into his pocket and flashed his credentials at Bradfield. 'Eric Blane' he said 'Oak Bluffs PD, Tony Leith probably told you I was coming'

Bradfield nodded his head in a robotic meandering way. Blane didn't think Bradfield had heard anything he'd just said to him.

Bradfield made his way into the house and sat down. Eric followed him closely.

'So we're looking for your wife and son, what's their names now, Jake and Claire right?' Eric said still standing.

'Have you found anything yet?' James asked, not answering Blane's question directly.

'Well no, we're still looking, trying to piece together the events that led up to their…disappearance' Blane deliberately paused before saying the last word, accentuating it as he did so. If Bradfield picked up on it, he certainly showed no sign of doing so.

'I know this probably sounds strange Mr. Bradfield, but has anybody thought of looking round the house, I mean this is a big place, you could get lost in here' Blane said.

Bradfield looked confused by this his brow furrowed as he thought about the question.

'Why on earth would they be here, that doesn't even make any sense?' Bradfield said, wearily. 'I think I would know don't you?'

Eric tried one more stab at getting to Mr. Bradfield for the sake of his hunch.

'Well the fact remains, in the majority of cases like this, turns out the person who reported it, had some kind of involvement in the first place' Blane said, accusingly 'now I'm not saying that's the case here' he lied 'but the fact remains, all avenues need to be looked at'

Bradfield looked at him with more life in his eyes than Blane had seen since he'd arrived there. He stood up and faced Blane, looking down on him due to his height.

'You really think I could have had anything to do with this?' he said, 'Really? I was at work and came home to an empty house and menacing phone call, when exactly do you think I managed this?' he asked. Blane was beginning to feel his hunch may have been a little misguided. Ever the stubborn mule though, he pushed on.

'You don't mind if I take a look round the house though do you Mr. Bradfield?' Blane retorted.

'Go ahead' Bradfield said slumping back down in the chair 'waste time when you could be finding my family, but if it satisfies your curiosity, then you go for a tour'

Blane smiled politely 'Thank-you, it will' he made his way over towards the dining room area as he said it and picked up the still open bottle of barely drunk red on the table. 'This is a nice vino' he said, really not to anyone other than himself. Bradfield sat and stared out the window looking forlorn and helpless.

Officer Jenny Clearwater entered the school gates and made her way over to the front office. The Edgartown Elementary was fairly small and quaint. It was near enough to the sea that the distinct aroma of the salty air drifted in on the faint breeze. It was a warm breeze on a gloriously hot day. The children were all in their classrooms now and the school was reasonably quiet given the number of noisy children it inhabited. One of the kids came out to the office, a small blonde girl and passed her classroom register over the desk to the grey haired woman sitting there. She thanked her and the little girl skipped off back to class. Jenny smiled to herself; she could hardly imagine that she had ever been that little.

The woman behind the desk looked up at her and smiled 'I imagine you're here about Jake Bradfield' she enquired, her smile shifting now 'that's a terrible business, we're all very concerned' she continued.

'Yes, yes it is' Jenny replied, 'but I am sure we will find him. I just need to speak to the head and find out if there is anything we need to know, anything that's been overlooked'

'Of course we'll help as much as we can, we just want Jake back safe and well' she said as she picked up the phone and dialed 'Yes, hello, Mrs. Kingsley, I have officer..' she stopped and placed her hand over the mouth piece 'sorry your name is?' she asked Jenny.

'Of course, it's Officer Jenny Clearwater' she answered. The woman went back to her conversation with the headmistress.

'Jenny Clearwater' she continued into the phone 'she's here about the Bradfield boy' she paused whilst she listened to Mrs. Kingsley on the other end of the phone. 'OK thank-you I will' she said before placing the telephone back in its resting place.

'She said she will be right out to see you' and at that the door to the left opened and a tall, raven-haired woman in her early fifties appeared.

'Officer Clearwater' she said, holding out her hand in greeting, which Jenny took gracefully 'I am Barbara Kingsley the headmistress of Edgartown Elementary School, please come in' she said as she beckoned Jenny into her office.

The oak wood office was quite poorly lit and only big enough to accommodate the desk and the two people inside.

'We're all deeply concerned about Jake, we've been told only that he and his mother have gone missing' she said, clearly digging for more information than she was about to get.

'That is correct' Jenny responded, with no intention of digressing any further information 'We're trying to trace Mrs. Bradfield's last known whereabouts' she continued 'we know she collected Jake from school at around 3.30pm but there is a gap following that which we're unable to fill'

Mrs. Kingsley nodded her head. 'Well I took the liberty to speak to some of the parents this morning and ask them if they saw anything unusual' she said 'there are quite a few playground cliques as is often the case and Claire Bradfield is usually with the same three or four people'

Jenny knew the benefit of having a busy body, which essentially is what Mrs. Kingsley was, onside. Whilst she meant well it was all too apparent that her motives were not driven by finding Jake as much as they were in finding gossip.

'OK thank-you and did anything of interest get mentioned?' Jenny enquired.

'Not really no, I'm afraid they all said she was her usual sprightly self, Jake was fine and off they went' Mrs. Kingsley answered. 'That's the funny thing about these playground cliques, they gather like hens and then as soon as they leave the playground, on their separate ways they go'

Jenny was disappointed; no information had come from this visit at all, well of any interest anyway.

'Right so really there was nothing out of the ordinary, that's a shame, I was hoping for something, I'm not sure what, but some kind of sign that something unusual was going on' Jenny said.

'Well there is one thing, probably not relevant but one of the mum's said Jake got a bit unhappy when Claire told him they were walking home' To Mrs. Kingsley it seemed like a throwaway comment but to Jenny, it had relevance.

'We were under the impression Mrs. Bradfield drives to school, in fact drove to school yesterday' Jenny said.

'No apparently not' Mrs. Kingsley replied 'she said the car wouldn't start, she was worried she wasn't going to get to school on time but someone had offered her a lift whilst she was walking' Jesus this could be the jackpot, Jenny thought.

'OK is there any idea on who that someone was?' Jenny asked, hopefully.

'Not as far as I am aware, probably one of the townsfolk. We all know each other round here' Jenny stood up and smoothed her clothing down. She knew that wasn't true, the town wasn't small enough for complete exclusivity, whether the headmistress wanted it perceived that way or not.

'Thank-you, Mrs. Kingsley, you have been a great help' she said.

'Is any of that relevant?' Mrs. Kingsley asked, excitedly.

'It may be yes, thank-you' Jenny said before exiting the office and making her way outside. She immediately got her mobile phone out and called Jed.

'Hey' she said as he answered 'tell Chief to get over to the Bradfield's, I'll meet you there. Claire never used the car to pick Jake up, it wouldn't start, she got a lift from someone' She listened to the other end and replied 'meet you there' before putting her phone away. The visit to the school hadn't been a waste of time after all.

Eric Blane finished touring the Bradfield residence just as Anthony, Jed and Jenny arrived. It was a nice house, he'd looked over it from top to bottom, but nothing seemed out of the ordinary and Bradfield certainly wasn't storing his wife and child's body in the attic. He saw Bradfield open the door and let the others in as he made his way down the stairs.

'I'm sorry' he said to Bradfield as he entered the living room 'I seem to have blocked your lavatory. It'll probably ease down in a minute but if it doesn't you may want to get some boiling water down there, works at home' he continued, without an ounce of shame. Bradfield looked disinterested with what was being said to him whilst the other three looked disgusted in equal measures.

'Your wife is one lucky lady Eric' Anthony said. Eric nodded in agreement, although he believed it one hundred percent.

'Can we look at your wife's car again?' Anthony directed his question to Mr. Bradfield.

'Of course' James answered, 'go ahead, you know where it is, the garage is open'

The four police officers walked outside and round to the garage, Eric unaware of what was going on but following all the same.

Anthony tried the door handle to the car and it was unlocked, so he popped the bonnet and opened it up. The engine was clean and the car was in good shape, all but for the various wires that had been clearly cut and sabotaged.

'Go and get Mr. Bradfield' Anthony said to nobody in particular. Jed went off.

'Someone has been fucking with that car in no uncertain terms' Eric said.

'She never did drive to school yesterday' Jenny answered. 'We know she was picked up by someone, but we don't know whom'

'Could be the same someone who did this' Anthony answered. 'Whatever is going on here, it certainly looks like this was a preconceived and well planned idea, but why?' he said looking perplexed.

Jed returned with Bradfield. Anthony pointed at the cars engine gesturing towards the sliced lead and cables.

'Someone did this before your wife picked Jake up from school, she had to walk yesterday' Anthony said 'She was picked up by someone while she was walking and dropped off at school to collect Jake, that much we know'

Bradfield stood and stared at the mess of cables in the engine.

'Your wife and your son were walking home from school' Anthony continued. 'We need to find whoever picked her up on the way there because it could be the same person who picked her up on the way home, or we could be looking for someone completely different, but either way, we have a lead'

'You have nothing' Bradfield said 'I have 2 days left or they're dead and you have a needle in a fucking haystack'

'I appreciate it's distressing for you, Mr. Bradfield' Jenny said, putting her hand on his arm, 'but we are further along than we were this morning, we'll find them, I promise'

Anthony interrupted. 'Can you think of anybody at all who you have seen hanging around, anybody who has been to the house lately who you didn't know or recognize? Even the smallest most irrelevant thing may be more important than you realize' he finished. Bradfield thought for a while.

'Well, no not really but we did have a party for Jake's Birthday the day before yesterday, there were plenty of people here then' he answered.

27

'OK this could be key' Blane said 'List them all, every one of them, no matter who it is and then we'll interview them all'

'When did your wife last use her car, as far as you're aware, Mr. Bradfield?' Anthony asked.

'Sunday morning before the party' he answered.

'So whoever did this' Blane said gesturing towards the car, 'did it Sunday then'

'Hang on though' Anthony had a thought 'surely your wife drove him to school yesterday morning as well?'

'No' Bradfield answered 'I drop him off on the way to work, she didn't need her car yesterday until she collected him again'

'Better get writing that list James' Anthony said, as Bradfield made his way back into the house to remember all of the party guests.

Anthony took Jenny by the arm and led her away from Jed and Eric.

'Listen' he said quietly 'I know it's hard but you can't make promises you may not be able to keep'

Jenny looked puzzled. 'What do you mean?'

'You promised him we'd find his wife and son and the fact is' Anthony answered 'we could yet be looking at a murder enquiry. Whoever did this to the car, it was pre-planned, they have a motive. We need to find what it is'

Anthony looked at the list of guests James had drawn up. There wasn't that many really, 10 kids, all dropped off by their parents and all collected later. The only 'outsiders' who had been there were the two guys who had erected the bouncy castle in the garden and the clown.

'OK we'll split into four and work our way through this list, there's not many on here' Anthony said.

'Actually it'll take a bit longer but I think we should do it in pairs' Eric said. 'If it turns out one of these people on here are responsible, do we want to be knocking on their door alone?'

It was a good point and Anthony hadn't considered it. To him the possibility that somebody living in this town may actually be a bona fide maniac was still hard to come to terms with. He kept waiting for

Jake and Claire Bradfield to make their way through the door. They were not going to.

'That's a good point Eric' Anthony replied 'You go with Jed and do the bottom half of the list, James has put all of the addresses on there, Jenny and I will do the top half' He proceeded to tear the list in half and give Eric his. 'Mark against any of these who seem as though they are acting suspiciously' Anthony said, as a side thought.

'Why can't you just search their houses and look around?' James asked, sitting over the other side of the room, looking out of the back window without making eye contact with anyway.

'We don't have time to get warrants from the court office for all of these people James' Jenny said.

'Anyway none of them are suspects here, they are just helping with our enquiries' Eric interrupted 'chances are, none of them know anything'

James looked up at Eric 'didn't stop you interrogating me and searching my house though did it' he said.

Eric didn't reply, James was right to a certain extent but he'd solved cases in the past based on hunches, even if those cases were minor compared to this one.

'Listen James' Anthony said 'none of us have any experience in this type of thing; it just doesn't happen here, you know that. We're doing all that we can I can assure you' James didn't reply as the four police officers rose and left the house.

He continued to sit their silently staring out of the window feeling nothing but helplessness. He knew the police were doing as much as they could but it didn't feel like enough. Time was moving and if the guy who had his family was serious, well, it didn't bare thinking about really. But what if he wasn't? It had been playing on James' mind for a while. He kept wondering, what if he didn't make a choice, would this man then let them go? Was he really prepared to murder two people for nothing? Who could do such a thing? It seemed beyond insane to James. The Chief was right of course, nothing like this had happened before. Perhaps, James thought, it would be an idea to get some help from the city. At that moment there was a knock on the door.

James went to answer it and outside stood a small, bespectacled man with brown curly hair.

'Walter Peabody' he said, holding out his hand.

'I don't have time for Salesmen today I'm afraid' James said, pushing the door closed as he did.

'I'm here to try and get some prints off the car' Walter replied before the door clicked back into place. James pulled it open again.

'Prints he asked. 'Yes, Eric Blane called me, I work over at Oak Bluffs forensics lab' Walter replied. He had a shrill, nasally New Jersey drawl.

'Oak Bluffs have a forensics lab?' James said 'You can't be that busy'

Walter laughed 'Not really no, I also work in the pathology lab as well and believe me, that's even worse. I'm a jack of all trades anyway. I'll do whatever is required of me' he said smiling.

James went outside and showed him round to the car before leaving Walter outside to do whatever it was he was going to do and made his way back in. As James walked into the house he realized the phone was ringing. He picked it up and said 'hello'

'Hello, Mr. Bradfield' the voice from the previous day spoke 'have you made your decision yet?'

James was enraged; this man was tormenting him, tormenting his wife, his child. He felt as though an internal explosion had detonated and screamed down the telephone. 'Give me my wife and son back, you fucking animal' he screamed.

The man on the other end said nothing for a few seconds.

'So no decision then?' he replied. James slumped to the floor, still holding the phone to his ear and began to sob.

'Please, please just give them back, they haven't done anything to you' he begged down the phone. The voice on the other end began to laugh and mimicked James in frightening and cold way

'*Please, please just give them back*' he mocked 'Why don't you grow a pair and make a choice, Mr. Bradfield, before you lose them both' The man said, returning to his normal menacing tone.

'Why are you doing this, I will give you anything you want, please, why, why are you doing this?' James asked again.

'Because, Mr. Bradfield, I can' the man replied. 'You have nothing you can give me, other than a choice in 48 hours' the line went dead as the man put the phone down.

James sat on the floor where he was, feeling light headed and dizzy. Suddenly, he got up and ran to the bathroom, vomiting profusely into the toilet, still blocked by Eric Blane's earlier visit.

Chief Anthony Leith and Jenny Clearwater stopped the police truck outside the Brubaker Brothers residence. As they did Anthony's phone rung and he pulled it out of its holster and answered it. He listened for a while and nodded before saying 'OK, try and remain calm' he listened again 'I will think about that' He put the phone away and looked at Jenny.

'He's called James again, told him he has 48 hours' Anthony looked grim 'he thinks we should involve the press in the city and get them to run a story on it' Jenny nodded her head.

'May reach more people than we can, what harm is there in it?' she answered.

'Just worried some hack will get hold of the story and turn it into something it's not' Anthony said 'last thing we need is having this psychotic antagonized by press manipulation, you know what they're like' Jenny nodded in agreement.

'Anyway' he continued 'we have people to interview this evening which may result in something positive. A lot can happen in two days' Anthony said, seemingly trying to convince himself if nobody else.

They climbed out of the truck and made their way up the path to the Brubaker's house. Anthony had known John and Andy Brubaker since school, the twins were the year below him but he'd always gotten on well with them. They'd done many different jobs since school and Andy used to be the local handyman, 'Handy Andy' they used to call him. Now though, the boys ran a successful business hiring out inflatable castles, to the local families for parties and the schools for fetes. Given the good weather Edgartown had most of the year, it had turned into a lucrative little business and was five years strong now. The boys were doing well for themselves, although looking at the disrepair their home was in and the overgrowth that was the front lawn, you'd have to wonder.

Andy and John had both been married and both divorced their wives within a year of each other. The two of them had children, who Anthony imagined had long since flown the nest. As the wives had left town and taken the kids with them, Anthony didn't know the full story. He knew

Andy had two boys and John two daughters, all of similar ages, but the guys had been divorced for probably fifteen years now. He hadn't seen those kids since then, not that they would be kids anymore. Andy opened the door and seemed genuinely surprised to see Anthony and Jenny standing there.

'Anthony Leith!' he said 'It's been a while, what brings you here?' he asked, with that same understandable twang of concern in his voice that anybody who answers the door to a police officer has, even if they're not guilty of anything.

'Can we come in please Andy?' Anthony said. Andy showed the two officers in and sat them down in the 'living' room. It was filthy. There were old pizza boxes on the sofa, old empty beer cans strewn all over the place and even a stack of Michelin tires in the corner of the room. The place was a wreck. Jenny thought they could do with a woman around the house, as long as it wasn't her. The place smelt awful, a mix of filth, sweat and testosterone.

'You did a party on Sunday' Anthony said, after finding somewhere relatively safe to sit.

'Yeah that's right, over at the Bradfield place' Andy replied 'what's happened? There were no accidents were there, they didn't tell us when we collected the inflatable, they said the kids had fun' Andy looked concerned.

'No, no accidents, nothing like that' Anthony said 'Mrs. Bradfield and her son have gone missing and we're just trying to trace their last known steps.'

Andy looked genuinely shocked and concerned.

'Jesus Christ, that's terrible' he answered wide eyed 'they're a nice family and that Mr. Bradfield gave us an extra twenty dollars as well' he said.

'Did you see anything odd at all when you were there on Sunday?' Jenny asked him. Andy thought for a while.

'No, nothing really, not that I would have noticed to be honest, we weren't there long, half hour tops each time. It's kind of hard to notice anything much when there are loads of excitable screaming kids running around, you know what I mean?' Andy said, smiling. As he did so he looked above Jenny's head at something on the wall. She turned around to see a picture of two girls and two boys playing on the sand, probably around eight or nine years old.

'Yours?' she asked him still looking at the pictures.

'The two boys are' he said, looking wistfully 'the girls are my brothers, we both had twins you know, what's the chances of that?' he said.

'Where are they now?' Jenny asked, not answering him.

'Ahh we got divorced sixteen years ago, me from my Bernie and John from Melissa, they got custody of the kids and went to live in the city,' Andy answered, he looked upset 'It's a shame really, they grow up quick enough as it is but when you only see them twice a year they grow up so much quicker. Then they get old enough that they don't even want to see you that many times either' he said, looking at the picture the whole time. 'My boys are twenty four now Anthony, can you believe that?' he said, diverting his eyes to the chief. Anthony raised his eyebrows and exhaled his breath.

'Where does it go aye Andy' he said clicking his thumb and index finger together 'gone, just like that.'

Andy nodded his head in agreement and looked back at the picture on the wall.

'You find that man's family Anthony, thing like that can destroy a man' he said, nodding his head in agreement at his own comment.

'We're trying Andy, we're really trying' Anthony said and then moving off the subject 'Where is John anyway?'

Andy broke his gaze from the picture on the wall and appeared to return to the real world.

'He's over at Frankie's bar, drinking his liver to death again no doubt' he answered. Anthony stood up and patted Andy on the shoulder.

'We may pop over and see him later' he said 'thanks for your time Andy.'

'No worries at all, wish I could have been some kind of help' he said rising from the litter strewn chair. He showed the two officers out and shut the door behind them returning back to the room they had just left. He picked up the handset to the old styled circular dial telephone and dialed a number. 'Hey John, it's me, you still over at Frankie's bar?' he said to his brother. 'OK, Chief Anthony Leith is going to be popping down to talk to you, you're not going to believe this, but that family we did the party for on Sunday, the wife and kid have gone missing.'

Chapter Five

Anthony and Jenny spoke while they made their way to their next destination, the home of Barry Monkwood, the local entertainer.

'Don't think he had anything to do with it' Jenny said, in regards to Andy Brubaker.

'Not a chance' Anthony replied, 'there's no way, he seemed genuinely shocked, although we will need to speak to his Brother as well' he continued.

'They live in a pig sty' Jenny remarked. She grimaced just at the thought of the place 'I feel like I need a shower now' she continued. Anthony laughed.

'Yeah, place could sure do with a Woman's touch' he said.

'Could do with being burnt down' she replied, which made him laugh so hard he held his stomach as he did. 'Seriously, how can people live like that?' she asked rhetorically.

'I tell you one thing' Anthony said 'whoever is behind this has a certain amount of organization and those two appear to be lacking that one element of function that's for sure'

Rain started to lightly sprinkle on the windscreen and Anthony looked up to see large cumulous nimbus clouds gathered above, like giant grey marshmallows filled with nothing more than water.

'There's a storm coming' he said 'we're due one as well, it's been hot again today' Edgartown suffered the occasional storm, usually a tremendous one when it came, over the summer months. It was often a blessed relief because it signaled the end of a particularly warm uncomfortable spell. Whilst the weather had been that way today, neither Jenny nor Anthony had noticed. They'd been so focused on trying to find something, anything, in relation to the disappearance of Mrs. Bradfield and her Son, that the weather hadn't really affected them. It usually drove Anthony mad sitting in his office in the stifling heat. Jenny felt awful for thinking it but actually having a case of note to work on was considerably more entertaining than the usual day to day banality of working in the Edgartown Police Department. If truth be told she had been considering the possibility of moving to the city and joining their police force recently. There was little to keep a young woman interested and attracted in such a small uneventful town. The two Police Officers arrived at Barry Monkwood's place little over five minutes later.

'Jesus I hope this guy isn't dressed as a clown' Anthony retorted as the truck drew to a halt.

'Why on earth not?' Jenny asked, laughing at the thought of it.

'Because I'm bothered by them, in fact no, I'm shit scared of them' he corrected himself. Jenny burst out laughing followed immediately by Anthony. To both of them laughing in the current situation felt wrong but at the same time it was as relief giving as the pending storm to be.

'Seriously it's not funny' he said, still laughing 'I've had a real issue with clowns since I was a kid'

'Why, what happened when you were a kid?' Jenny asked, through her laugher. Anthony thought for a second.

'I really don't know' he said 'I must have blocked it from my memory. They creep me out anyway clowns, as do people who dress up as them, what's that all about really?' he said.

'Oh please, this guy does it to make kids happy, that's a nice way to be isn't it? Jenny said.

'Well I bet he makes as many happy as he does mess them up in their head for life' Anthony said.

Unclasping their seat belts Anthony and Jenny composed themselves and climbed out of the car. Barry Monkwood's house was very well kept and in complete contrast to the abode they had just left. It was pristine and in an obviously cared for condition. The front lawn was well trimmed and there were an array of beautiful flowers scattered all over it. A child's red tricycle was all that separated the lawn from its other finery. Anthony felt the house was idyllic. He turned to look behind him, a terrific view of the sea was there to behold on a daily basis. The rolling black thunder clouds which filled the skyline loomed above ominously.

Jenny knocked on the door and a smart, well-dressed man opened it. Fortunately he was not dressed as a clown.

35

'Can I help you?' he asked, looking puzzled.

'Barry Monkwood?' Jenny asked him as Anthony stood behind, seemingly waiting for a clown to jump out and say 'boo.'

'Yes' Barry answered, looking puzzled further still. 'What's wrong?'

'I'm Chief Anthony Leith this is my Deputy, Jenny Clearwater' Anthony said, 'may we come in?'

Mr. Monkwood nodded his head, 'Of course, of course, come through' he said. The house was light and airy with delicate pink walls and lemony décor. The living room smelt perfumed and Anthony observed the plug in air freshener in the wall. Now this was a house with a feminine touch. There were pictures of Mr. Monkwood with a woman and a female child, presumably his daughter, adorning practically every wall. The house smacked of family as you walked in, indeed this was a home and not a house at all. Mr. Monkwood gestured towards the sofas. 'Can I get either of you a drink?' he asked. They both shook their heads and politely replied in the negative.

'You performed at a party on Sunday?' Anthony asked. Mr. Monkwood thought for a while and grabbed an apple from the fruit bowl situated on the varnished coffee table as he did. He took a bite out of it with a loud crunch, the juice spraying in various different directions like a mini sprinkler.

He reached to his right and got a diary from the sofa side table and opened it. He nodded his head.

'That's right, the Bradfield's. Hmm that one didn't go down too well' Mr. Monkwood said smiling.

'How do you mean, not too well?' Jenny asked.

'Well, you kind of know when they're enjoying it, I've been doing this a long while' Mr. Monkwood said, his glasses perched on the end of his nose. 'I got the feeling that some of the kids were a bit scared, clowns can be scary things really, they're a bit hit and miss sometimes, you know what I mean?' Anthony nodded his head vicariously; he knew exactly what Mr. Monkwood meant.

'Not a big fan of them myself if I'm honest' Anthony said. Mr. Monkwood laughed.

'I'll let you into a little secret, neither am I' he replied, taking another bite out of the apple 'anyway, what's the problem, I haven't upset anyone that much surely?' Mr. Monkwood asked.

'I'm afraid Mrs. Bradfield and her son Jake have gone missing,' Jenny said.

'That's terrible' Mr. Monkwood said, barely pausing. 'Do you have any idea what has happened to them?'

'We're just following up as much as we can at the moment but no, nothing has really risen as being an obvious motive at the moment' Anthony said

'Did you speak much to the Bradfield's on Sunday?' he continued.

'No, not really, they booked me in a few weeks ago and I turned up as 'Bozzo' which is my clown of course' Mr. Monkwood answered, 'did some magic tricks, made a fool of myself and put some balloon animals together for the kids. Standard stuff really'

'You have a daughter, Mr. Monkwood?' Anthony said, gesticulating towards one of the photographs, 'bet she loves daddy the clown'

Mr. Monkwood laughed 'Jane is ten now and no, she hates it, I've done a few of her friends birthday parties and she's always overwhelmingly embarrassed by me unfortunately' he said.

'She's at school I take it?' Anthony asked.

'No she's not, she's in the city with her mum at the moment' Monkwood said, taking a further bite out of the nearly depleted apple.

'Oh I see, may I ask why?' Anthony responded.

'My wife, Sandra, her Mother is ill at the moment, really ill actually, being treated for the big C. She doesn't have long left' Mr. Monkwood replied 'the school have been really good, given Jane special dispensation and a few weeks off to see her Gran, probably for the last time so Sandra has taken her with her, it's a sad time' he said, taking another bite of the apple and crunching it loudly.

'You didn't want to go as well then?' Jenny asked him, slightly repulsed as he chewed with his mouth open. The contents rotated like a food filled washing machine in her face.

'Would have but someone has to stay here and keep the bills paid don't they' Mr. Monkwood smiled as he said this 'and between you and me, I'm not a big fan of the wife's mother and neither is she of me. Archetypal Mother In-Law syndrome you could call it' he laughed as he said this, the bits of apple still stuck to his tongue and teeth laughing with him. He glanced at his watch 'Oh I have to get made up, I have a party this afternoon' he said looking out of the window 'I hope that weather holds off.'

'I don't think it will' Anthony said ' anyway I think we've covered everything but if anything at all springs to mind let us know, even if you think it may not be important' he concluded stereotypically.

'Oh I will' Mr. Monkwood said 'really is awful, you don't expect that here do you? I don't know what I would do if that was my Janey I'll tell you'

The two police officers made their way to the front door and Anthony shook Mr. Monkwood's hand, which was beaded with droplets of sticky apple.

'Thank-you for your time sir' Jenny said, as the two officers made their way out of the house.

'Anytime' Mr. Monkwood said, as he closed the door behind them. Taking one last bite of the apple he tossed it into the waste basket in the living room doorway and made his way upstairs. The bedroom he and his wife shared was as airy and bright as the rest of the house. He opened the wardrobe and got the Clown outfit hanging there out and hung it from the top of the bedroom door.

Sitting down at the make-up mirror he opened the bag. He wondered how many men had a separate bag of make-up to their wives. Monkwood began to plaster on the make-up. Swathing his face in white and then accentuating his mouth with a downturned smile in red lipstick. He was the perpetually unhappy clown, the depressed clown, the miserable clown. Bozzo was an idiot clown. He smiled at his own reflection, the smile giving a confused and contradictory appearance to the sad joker he had painted himself as.

Anthony and Jenny drove away from Monkwood's house the rain now falling heavily on the car, hitting it with the sounds of a million marbles rattling in a bag.

'Jesus that is going to be some storm' Anthony said, just as lightning split the sky and a distant rumble was heard overheard.

'Yeah it is' Jenny answered 'you can smell it coming' Anthony knew exactly what she meant as well. There was a distinct aroma in the air every time they had a storm. It was impossible to describe or put your finger on but when that smell rose up, a storm was coming and everybody knew it. The smell was not that earthy odor you always seemed to get when the rain fell after a dry period, it was something else, almost electric in the air.

'What did you think of him, the clown?' Anthony asked her.

'He seemed nice enough; I don't think what is going on has anything to do with the guests at that party on Sunday' Jenny said 'it's just coincidence'

'I think you are almost certainly right but there was something I didn't like about him' Anthony said.

'Really?' Jenny seemed surprised 'like what?'

'Well it was the way he was slightly nonchalant about the mother in law, it didn't seem to bother him a great deal' Anthony replied 'like he didn't care.'

'Really how many men aren't keen on their wife's mother?' Jenny responded 'he probably isn't overly concerned if he has the type of relationship most guys have with their mother in-law you can imagine the grief she probably gives him just for being a clown'

It was a good point. 'Yes, you're probably right there as well' Anthony said. A loud crack of thunder split the evening as nightfall began to draw in, making both officers jump.

'I love a good storm,' Anthony said.

'But clowns scare you!?' Jenny replied, laughing.

Chapter Six

Bozzo the sad clown took the kitchen knife and sliced the sandwich before him in two. Placing it on a plate he then transferred the food to a wooden lap tray. On the side of the tray was a bowl of sausage rolls, a smaller bowl of crisps, a bottle of cola and a glass. Bozzo seemed destined to have himself a small feast but his sad smile still remained.

He picked up the tray and made his way down the hall breathing in the delightful aroma of the plug in air freshener, but this didn't make him feel any happier. He opened a door and made his way downstairs to the basement.

The child and the woman were sitting in the chairs he had tied them to, before the interfering officers had arrived. He put the tray on the floor and removed Mrs. Bradfield's gag from her mouth.

'You fucking animal' she screamed in his face 'un-gag my son now'

'I apologies, Mrs. Bradfield, but in less than 48 hours this will be all over, so be patient please' Bozzo said.

'What do you want, what are you asking my husband for? We don't have loads of money, he can't pay you' she shouted at him.

He lent towards Jake who flinched, his wide eyes transfixed on Bozzo. The clown put his hand out and quickly removed the gag from Jake's mouth.

'I want to go home' Jake said and started crying, looking at his Mother for some kind of assistance or reassurance. She was in a position to offer neither.

'I know you do son' the clown said 'you're only going to be here another couple of days and that is a Bozzo promise' he continued.

'What makes you so sure?' Mrs. Bradfield asked 'I'm telling you my husband cannot pay you whatever it is you're asking for'

'Your husband, Mrs. Bradfield, can do exactly what it is he is being asked to do, have no fear, there is nothing stopping him from carrying out his orders' Bozzo said, looking deeply into her eyes.

'What have you asked him for' she shouted again, 'what do you want him to do?' she said.

'He just has to make a decision' the clown answered 'how hard can that be?'

'What decision, what have you asked him to do?' she pleaded to know.

'Just know that this will all be over in two days' he said.

'I'm going to untie your hands now so you can eat, if there is any nonsense from you then I am taking it out on him' he continued, gesturing towards Jake.

'I don't want to eat, I'm not hungry,' Claire said.

'You are though aren't you son?' the clown said to Jake. Jake nodded his head in agreement. Children, whatever the problem, will always eat.

He lent forward and untied Jake's hands and then sat there while he ate the sandwich. The clown who had seemed like fun at his Birthday party only days before stared menacingly as Jake chewed. No sooner had Jake finished his sandwich, the clown was retying him to the chair.

Looking at Claire, Bozzo the Clown spoke again 'I'll be back later to untie you both so you can sleep' he said, gesturing towards the two foldaway camp beds they had been sleeping on.

'Why are you doing this to us, what have we done to you?' she begged to know.

'You have done nothing to me, Mrs. Bradfield' the clown answered quietly.

'So why then, why do it, why not just let us go, please?' she pleaded again.

'I can't, I'm sorry' he said, seeming to genuinely mean it 'I have to do this' he said, as he got up and made his way up the steps towards the basement exit. He looked back at both of them.

'Please don't make too much noise down here, screaming and hollering like you did last night' he told them 'it's a complete waste of time. Nobody can hear you other than me' He shut the door behind him and Claire heard the key turn in the door as he locked it.

She tried not to cry, so as not to upset Jake. She needed to be strong for him. They would get out of this.

The four police officers made their way into Edgartown's most favorite eatery 'The Shack' It was standard fair, burgers, fries, battered chicken, steaks, the type of food a lifetime's worth of which would shorten your life's span by a considerable length. In other words the type of place Eric Blane would have his breakfast, lunch and dinner if he could afford to. Anthony, Jenny, Jed and Eric squeezed their way into one of the red coloured booths, Eric literally wedging himself into place. Jenny wondered to herself if he would be able to get out, after he'd finished eating.

The staff gathered around one of the tables and sang 'Happy Birthday' in an over the top and embarrassing manner to one of the unsuspecting patrons. The man sank further into his seat willing the booth to swallow him up as his highly amused friends surrounded him laughing.

The four Police Officers looked at the menus, Eric's eyes positively bursting out of his head, he wanted to order everything.

'I'm starving' Eric said 'I haven't eaten all day' he rubbed his gargantuan gut half hanging over the top of the table whilst the rest rippled below.

'You had two burgers at lunchtime' Jed said, looking stunned.

'Yeah but that was hours ago, you can't count that now' Eric said, meaning every word of it.

'So today has been a complete washout then?' Anthony said 'I don't think any of us really held out much hope of digging anything up, it was a shot in the dark.'

'To be honest with you, we're looking for a needle in a haystack' Eric replied, 'and I still have a question mark over that Bradfield guy.'

'You're flogging a dead horse there,' Anthony said. 'Let it go.'

'I have, but I'll be reminding you of this when I'm proven right' Eric replied nonchalantly.

A waitress came over, chewing gum and looking thoroughly dissatisfied with her job. You could tell from the vacant look in her eyes, life hadn't panned out as she'd hoped it would. Anthony knew that feeling only too well.

42

Are you ready to order?' she asked, disinterested either way. Anthony looked around at everybody and with the exception of Eric, nobody was. He, of course, ordered more food than a normal human being would be prepared to consider. The waitress took the lengthy order down and read it back to him.

'Can you give the rest of us five minutes please?' Anthony said. She looked at the order she'd just written down.

'Right, so this isn't for all of you?' she questioned. She looked at Anthony and then she looked at Eric, her eyes moving down to his extraordinarily large midriff before nodding her head and saying 'I see' and walking away.

'What does she mean 'I see'? Eric asked, looking down at himself, presumably seeing nothing more than a tanned Adonis.

'I think there is a chance this guy has taken them into the city but how would we know?' Jenny changed the subject, continuing the conversation from earlier. 'I really think we should consider the possibility of contacting the press, the Massachusetts Times can run a story and get this out there' she continued. They all thought about it in tandem.

'It's a good idea' Jed said 'can't hurt can it?'

'But it has been known to hurt in some cases, where the press antagonize them to the extent they end up doing something to prove a point' Anthony said.

'They're probably dead already' Eric said, without really seeming to care if that was the case 'guarantee you this moron has chopped them up and buried them somewhere already, we'll never see them again' he continued and then, as a side thought 'I wonder how long they'll be with dinner, I'm going to waste away here' Anthony looked at Jed who looked back at Jenny, sitting opposite him.

'I don't think that has happened for one minute' Anthony said, getting slightly agitated by Eric's attitude. He'd began to regret asking him for assistance, he hadn't really done anything of value in the past day anyway. 'This guy is playing a game, God knows why but he is and he's made the rules of this game clear, he wants to play it out' he concluded.

'We'll see' Eric responded, still looking at the menu, despite having ordered 'the next two days will pass and we'll hear nothing, these threats won't be carried out'

'Anyway, about going to the press,' Jenny interrupted 'I think it is something we have to really seriously consider, we're running out of time' and she was right, if the threats were genuine, then time was of prime importance. Anthony felt as though they were doing James Bradfield and his family a disservice sitting there about to eat dinner. At that moment the waitress came back, still chewing on her gum and still looking like she'd rather be standing in front of a train than right here, right now.

'So, you made your minds up yet?' she asked them, standing with one hand on her hip while the other clutched her order pad, the pen slipped through the looped rings at the side.

'Yes, I have' Anthony answered, and he had, but not just about what to eat, he'd also decided what to do. Jenny was right, it was time to involve the press.

Chapter Seven

The brown shoes made their way to the kitchen draw and pulled out a knife, a large gleaming weapon of a blade, the type that couldn't really do anything other than seriously hurt, maim and kill. It was too large to prepare vegetables with; in fact, it was as big as an axe, huge. The brown shoed owner looked down on it, holding it with both hands, both large hands. Whoever this was, it was male. He made his way down some stairs and then into a basement. There was a woman tied to a chair and a small boy, also tied up. The man put the knife down and was suddenly holding a gun. 'I'm sorry' he spoke 'but the time is now up' he aimed the gun at the woman who attempted to scream through the gag around her mouth. Then without warning he diverted the attention of the gun barrel to the boy and cold bloodily shot him in the face. The red strew of blood splattered all over the wall behind as the force of impact threw the boy backwards in the chair, his lifeless corpse toppling to the floor leaving his still seated body laying still, his feet momentarily twitching towards the assassin. The Woman's sobbing; muffled screams were momentary as the murderer proceeded to do the same to her, shooting her not once, but twice in the head. The level of blood was twice as much, but her silence doubly as quick. The man walked over and looked into her lifeless eyes.

Terrence Denton shot bolt upright in bed, his body ringing with sweat. It was as though he'd had a shower. When would the dreams end? He had never had such vivid, awful recurring dreams before but this was the third night in succession his sleep had been frighteningly awakened with this one and it was beginning to concern him. He felt the dream had some kind of significance, but didn't know why. It just felt so real.

Anthony opened his bedroom curtains and the sun gleamed through, invading his sleepy eyes and senses to the maximum. The storm of the previous day had turned into a damp squib and hadn't delivered on its promise. Anthony loved a thunderstorm, got off on them almost and the imminent arrival of a cracking metrological display being replaced by a light shower, a couple of rumbles and a general passing was, to say the least, disappointing. Now he was met this morning by the usual glare of the sun. He was sleeping in the spare room, mainly because he wasn't sleeping at all. His wife's patience for his constant tossing and turning had more than ran out and she cordially requested he go elsewhere before she stabbed him. She meant that in jest, he was almost sure. He'd slept better last night than he had for a few days but even then it had been interrupted. It wasn't that the case was playing on his mind and interrupting his sleep patterns, not at all. He'd felt this way now for a while. He put it down to being depressed and over the last few months his sleep deprivation had gotten much worse. The current case probably didn't help and he was only too aware of how time was running out, if the abductor kept his word.

Anthony dialed the number for the Massachusetts Times and was immediately answered by a pleasant speaking woman. He explained to her who he was and that he needed to speak to someone and in moments he was speaking to a gentleman.

'What can I do for you officer?' the man asked, instantly appearing to have an arrogant swagger to the way he spoke. Anthony may have been wrong and he was acutely aware of his lack of impartiality when it came to the press but even so, this guy's voice and tone of speaking instantly got his back up.

'We have an issue here in Edgartown, we thought you may be interested in running a report on it' Anthony said.

'With all due respect officer' the man replied 'we're not interested in running a piece on who's stolen who's rhododendron or who's boat clipped someone else's, you know what I'm saying?' the reporter asked sarcastically. Anthony didn't bite, it was obvious the reporter had an overwhelming sense of self-importance in comparison to the so called little town folk of Edgartown, or Martha's Vineyard in general, for that matter.

'A woman and her son have been abducted' Anthony responded, feeling some self-satisfaction and vindication at the same time.

'Oh, I see' the voice on the other end responded, sounding instantly humbled and equally as interested 'I'll get someone over to you guys right away. In fact, I may even come myself, it's unusual to get any kind of worthwhile story out of you lot' he continued.

'And you are whom?' Anthony asked. There was a short pause before the man responded 'I'm Mickey Henderson' it was Anthony's turn to feel humble. Mickey Henderson was the most highly regarded reporter in Massachusetts and one of the most highly acclaimed. Equally as notorious for his arrogance as he was his excellence.

'Out of interest' Mickey said 'how do you know they've been abducted?' he asked.

'Because the man responsible has given the husband 72 hours to choose which one he kills' Anthony responded.

'I'm leaving now' Mickey said, before Anthony was met with the tone of a disconnected telephone, ringing in his ears.

Mickey Henderson stood at the port of Woods Hole for the ferry to Martha's Vineyard. Although there was only a small stretch of water between Cape Cod and the Vineyard, about 7 miles to be precise, it wasn't the easiest place to get to. The ferries were infrequent at best but today Mickey's luck was in. He'd only been waiting for minutes when the next transport arrived ready to take him over. He quite liked the Vineyard, it was a decent place to go if you ever fancied a quiet retreat but he'd not been there for five years or so. He boarded the ferry and stood out on the deck looking overboard at the sea, the Atlantic Ocean always looked so much more foreboding when you were completely surrounded by it. From the shore, it was as pleasant and unassuming as any sea scape in the world but on a small boat, looking down on it from above, it was menacing and life threatening. Once he arrived at Chappaquiddick he'd then have to get the ferry to Edgartown.

Mickey Henderson puffed frantically on another cigarette. He'd fast turned into a heavy drinking chain smoking hack since he'd been with the Times. He wasn't concerned by this or indeed ashamed, being part of the press seemed to entail certain stereotypical traits and Henderson had no problem adhering to any of them.

47

He breathed in the fresh sea air as the ferry trundled over the water, spilling out spumes of foam and froth from either side. He could feel the salt drying on his face, it was a good feeling, to get away from the dirt and smog of the city.

Henderson thought about what the Chief of Police had said to him. Two people missing in Edgartown. Obviously they'd been kidnapped, rather than disappeared off the face of the earth without a trace. He'd drawn that conclusion from the fact he'd been asked to report on the incident in the first place.

As soon as Henderson had put the phone down he immediately cleared it with his Editor, who'd wanted, no demanded, he get straight over to Edgartown. In his own words 'Jesus, get the story, nothing but nothing ever happens over there' and he was right. Edgartown and in fact Martha's Vineyard as a whole were a complete safe haven. Henderson was looking forward to the story, it would make a change to have somewhere to write about that wasn't focused on the grime and shit in his own back yard.

Anthony Leith looked out across the ocean as he awaited Mickey Henderson's arrival. He wasn't sure at all what the involvement of the press would achieve, other than to get the story out there and make people aware, possibly giving them some leads. At the same time though he was concerned about how the reporter would reflect his town, how the story would sound and whether it would strike fear, which was not the intention, into the locals.

Time was fast running out for Mrs. Bradfield and her Son and Anthony realized that there was a chance this could all be some awful elaborate hoax just as there was it would all end in bloodshed. He was concerned however, with a number of things that had become apparent in the past couple of days. The most obvious concern was how out of their depth both himself and Eric Blane were. In all their years on the Vineyard's respective forces neither of them had ever had to deal with anything close to this, close to being so deadly serious.

What also bothered him was the complete lack of understanding they had of the whole thing. There was no apparent motive, nothing James Bradfield could think of that resonated with being any kind of hatred towards him or his family. The Bradfield's were to all intents and purposes a well liked family who never upset or were a concern towards anybody. Both Anthony and Jenny had interviewed the few neighbors that were dotted around them and all were genuinely shocked and concerned. What could he do, ask to search every house? He guessed it was an option but it seemed extreme to say the least and he wondered if Jenny was right, they may not even be on the island, in fact if it were him that was responsible, he'd make sure they weren't.

Mickey Henderson arrived and clambered off the boat. Wearing a long beige trench coat and emanating the stench of stale cigarettes, Anthony was instantly vindicated of his stereotypical perception of the tabloid reporter. Henderson's ruddy complexion spoke volumes about his regular inebriation as did the subtle, yet noticeable yellowing of the whites of his eyes.

Anthony drove him to Edgartown's local café for a pastry and a coffee whilst they discussed the case. The chief made it very clear to Henderson that there was to be no antagonistic writing about the abductor. They did not know enough about him to assume he wouldn't react adversely to such a tactic. Chain smoking his way through the discussion Henderson made copious amounts of notes, nodding his head, listening intently and generally saying very little. He wanted the story.

'Can I meet Mr. Bradfield?' Henderson asked, once the note taking had been finished.

'I don't think that's a particularly good idea' Anthony said, shaking his head.

'Listen, I appreciate the guy is probably distraught, but the fact remains, people love a good compassionate side to every story' Henderson said 'and let's not underestimate the effect that could have on your killer if he reads that as well' he paused to take a mouthful of coffee, which by now was stone cold.

'He's not a killer, he hasn't killed anybody' the Chief said, slightly perturbed by the suggestion.

'Well if he hasn't killed them yet, then he certainly intends to kill one, if not both of them' Henderson said. 'Have you thought about what you intend to do when that happens, you know, what your approach will be, because this is a whole new ball game once that scenario lands?' Truth is the Chief hadn't thought about it, he hadn't

49

wanted to. In his ideal world, and Edgartown was among other things, an idea world, he and the team would save the day. The other prospect he couldn't bear to think about but, Henderson was right, the clock was ticking and time was running out.

'Well let's just hope you're piece draws him out or appeals to somebody who saw something they didn't realize was relevant at the time' Anthony said.

'Well it won't draw him out, the guy has a plan, has a reason' Henderson said 'so don't hang your hat on that one but it may jog a memory or two' Henderson paused as if he was thinking 'but you have no idea what you're going to do if the shit hit's the fan here do you?' Anthony didn't answer, he just continued looking at the reporter. Henderson didn't need him to answer, he knew full well. This wasn't Leith's usual stolen bike situation.

'Anyway, I really think you should take me to meet Mr. Bradfield' Henderson said, moving the course of the conversation. He didn't want to lose the Chief now and he could sense he was getting to him. The raw nerve had been hit with the force of a hammer on a tiny nail.

The two men made their way out of the café and into the Chiefs truck. The radio station quietly played some old Genesis track in the background.

'I love a bit of Genesis' Henderson said as they pulled away, attempting to make some small talk.

The chief nodded his head 'They're OK I guess' he wasn't that keen on them if he was honest, he found their music trite and uninteresting but he played along with the small talk just to be polite to his guest.

'They were more than alright, great band, great live band as well, you ever see them?' Henderson seemed pleased he'd stumbled upon someone who seemingly liked the band he'd loved forever.

'No, never did' Anthony said, no longer interested in the small talk.

'Don't suppose you get off the island much aye chief?' Henderson probed, 'doubt you'd want to either, it's a quaint little place.'

It was funny, Anthony had never really thought about it but in all his life, with the exception of the trips across the water to

Massachusetts or Cape Cod, he had never vacationed 'away' from the Vineyard. Realizing it now seemed strange, somewhat sad. To the Chief it was just another example of an area of his life he had managed to allow to waste away and fall from his grasp.

'You know I've never actually got away from the Vineyard' Anthony answered him 'never had a holiday really, because being here is in a way like being on holiday' he continued, lying to himself. Henderson nodded his head in agreement. 'I can see that, but still be nice to go somewhere different, there are a lot of places out there' he replied, still nodding his head. The Chief realized he wasn't nodding in agreement but nodding at the song on the radio, much to his annoyance.

'Maybe once this case is over I'll catch a vacation with the wife, visit Europe or something' Anthony said, suddenly feeling an air of beleaguered optimism.

'Well I can see this case running some first' Henderson said, looking out of the window.

'How do you mean, running some?' Anthony answered, 'I think whatever is happening here finishes either way tomorrow'

'Yeah I hope so' Henderson answered, still looking at the view of Edgartown as it flashed past the passenger window in a hazy blur 'I have reported on enough of these types of people in my time to know one thing for sure, these things never, and I mean never, go the neat and tidy way you think they will' Henderson replied, fixing his gaze back on the chief. Not for the first time today, Anthony didn't answer. He left his eyes transfixed on the road ahead and then using the buttons on the steering column, indiscreetly switched the volume of the radio up a notch.

'This the local radio station?' Henderson asked in a disinterested, talking for the sake of it manner.

'Yes, Edgartown CRFM' Anthony answered, again pleased the conversation had diverted. He really didn't want to think too negatively about the Bradfield case, he was a firm believer in positive thinking breeding positive reward.

'Edgartown CRFM' Henderson repeated, to himself rather than the Chief 'CR for Community Radio I guess?' he said.

'Yep' Anthony answered, completely unaware of where Henderson was trying to take the conversation.

'You'd think you would have used the local radio station to make this public and get to people quicker, rather than us' Henderson said, re-directing his gaze back out of the passenger window. Anthony said nothing again, but he could feel his insides churn as he seethed internally. Why hadn't he thought of that? Why hadn't Jenny or the others? He felt foolish, some out of town hack was basically telling him how to do his job and what was worse is, he was right.

'Anyway, it'll be in the papers tomorrow and we'll get to people out of the Vineyard so you're going to reach a bigger audience with it' Henderson said, as if he was trying to make the Chief feel better about his oversight. It didn't work though and as they arrived at the Bradfield residence he couldn't help but again think he had let James Bradfield down, massively.

'You have a police computer, you know, that connects to the wider database?' Henderson asked as they arrived.

'Of course we do' Anthony asked, somewhat snappier than he'd intended to be.

'Anything interesting come up when you ran the locals names through it, or Mr. Bradfield's?' Henderson asked, inquisitively.

'No nothing at all, everybody seems pretty clean around here' Anthony lied. He hadn't even done something as simple as that, he genuinely didn't feel the need. Again though, Henderson was right. In their attempt to try and do as much as they could, the four police officers had missed the obvious actions. They had all failed to dot the I's and cross the T's but the fact remained that Anthony was the one leading the case. The responsibility to ensure everything was done correctly was his and to an extent Eric's. Neither of them had and now time was ever more so of the essence.

The two men disembarked from the car and made their way up the steps to the Bradfield house, steps that to the Chief were becoming all too familiar. He just wished he was climbing them with better news. He noticed as he climbed them that the wood on each step was cracking and deteriorating, mirroring the occupier inside. Anthony didn't need to knock, the front door was wide open.

'James' he called out, standing by the front door. There was no answer. The Chiefs heart began to pound in his ears and he was suddenly aware of the stickiness of his shirt collar around his neck.

The prickly feeling of the newly grown hair from his unshaven face felt as though it was an irritant.

'Go back to the car' he instinctively ordered Henderson 'something is not right'. Pulling the gun from its holster Anthony clasped the handle as if his life depended on it. He watched his fingers tremble as his foot raised and kicked open the door and held the gun, straight armed, in front of him. The Chiefs hands were sweaty and clammy and he could feel his index finger slip on the trigger. His breathing became acutely heavy as Henderson looked on from the car.

Henderson watched as the chief walked into the hallway and for the first time since he'd arrived at the Vineyard he began to feel real fear. From his top pocket he pulled out a weapon of his own. It was the Dictaphone he'd used all day to record his interview with Chief Anthony Leith and now he was recording himself, telling the recorder exactly what was unfolding in front of him. For an age all Henderson could hear was the sea battering the shore behind him and the occasional menacing core of a seagull swooping overhead. The sun blazed down on the back of his neck, magnified by the car window, beginning to burn but Henderson's position was immovable. He was not and would not take his eyes from the front of that house. If anything happened at all, Henderson would make sure he saw and heard it before anything else. A burnt neck was something he'd get over in a few days; a bullet in the head however was not so likely.

Henderson began to think of an escape route as the prolonged silence from the house in front continued. He had always found, more than anything else, that silence often had a way of striking fear into a man more than any sound ever could. Darkness was the same and the two put together, they were for him the epitome of fear itself.

Planning his escape route Henderson momentarily glanced at the ignition, realizing to his dismay that the Chief had the keys with him. Like every bad horror film he'd ever seen, there was no easy escape. He felt as though he had been driven straight into the worst cliché imaginable. Whilst Henderson focused on the interior of the car he realized he'd lost the attention of the house, which continued to watch over him unflinchingly. In that instant Henderson became aware of someone, a figure, standing in the doorway of the house.

His peripheral vision watched as his eyes looked in practically the opposite direction. Time seemed to stop for him, cease almost completely and Henderson was aware of his every sense. The smell of the sea air climbed up the walls of his nostrils and sent a message of resonance to his brain and his taste buds became inactive as his saliva glands shut down. His throat was dryer than the Nevada dessert and his stomach churned with the sudden spasm of nausea. All of these sensations and awareness's were apparent in their entirety and yet in reality took a mere second or two to divulge their information.

'It's OK, he was just sleeping' the chief said from the doorway.

Henderson's eyes adjusted to the shape in the doorway and he struggled to stifle his relief at his minds realization that it was just the chief standing there. Standing in the cold light of day, Henderson felt momentarily silly at how his rationale had been so quickly overtaken by fear.

'James is happy to speak to you' Anthony continued, completely oblivious to the fact that Henderson had just a moment before, been relatively certain some kind of human monster had been hiding and waiting to attack.

Henderson vacated the car and followed the Chief into the house and for the next hour interviewed James Bradfield.

He was intrigued by how the kidnapper called at 6pm every day and had wanted to stay for that evenings anticipated call. However, it was vital Henderson got back and had the story typed and pressed in order to make the following day's front page. Tomorrow was, after all, the alleged D-Day.

Henderson bid his goodbyes, thanked both Bradfield and the Chief for their hospitality and wished the former well and good luck, reassuring him the story would have a positive effect. Off Henderson went to make the short journey back to the City and with any luck, run a story that would shed some more light on exactly what was going on and hopefully resonate with somebody on some level, at least that is what the Chief was praying for.

The Clown sat in his sad make-up, loudly devouring an apple. The smart living room looked the same as it always did, bright and cheery but for the sad clown, sitting alone on the upholstery. Barry

Monkwood wasn't just sad on the outside, of course, he was sad on the inside as well. His two captives sat helpless in the dank, dreary basement of his light and breezy house completely unaware that one, if not both, would be dead in just twenty four hours. He took another bite out of the apple and felt overwhelmingly miserable. It didn't seem fair that the fate of those two helpless people hung in the hands of somebody else and yet that was exactly how it was. He wished he could just let them both go and pretend it had never happened, he really did. But Barry Monkwood knew, that could never happen, the game had to be played out the way it was meant to be because, when all was said and done, those were the rules. As his dad had always said, 'rules is rules' and as Barry knew only too well a game can only have a winner if it is played out in the correct way and he was certainly doing his bit. His teeth sliced into the apple again and chewed away, looking down at the remaining core he saw a small, wriggling maggot, suddenly unearthed from its fruitful tomb, revealed in the brightly sunlit room. Barry felt repulsed and annoyed. He quickly made his way into the kitchen and threw the remaining piece of fruit in the bin and spat the remnants from his mouth into the kitchen sink. He was annoyed because over the last few days all he'd been able to stomach was apples, it was all he could keep down. Now he felt put off by them as well.

Making his way back into the front room, Barry Monkwood looked at the clock. It was one minute away from being exactly twenty four hours until Mr. Bradfield had to make his decision. He picked up the receiver and began to dial the number, being sure to withhold his before he did. He hoped against hope that Mr. Bradfield had made a decision and would bring everybody's nightmare to an end.

Chapter Eight

Anthony made his way into the store to pick up the Massachusetts Times. He was interested to see what Henderson had written. There were a number of people milling around outside, as was often the case. All of them though were reading the newspaper, the same newspaper, the Massachusetts Times.

As Anthony made his way into the shop only a few customers remained. He bent down to pick up a copy of the newspaper for himself, when a rolled up one gently tapped him on the shoulder.

'Good idea this' Barry Monkwood said, unfurling the newspaper and showing the front page to the Chief.

'Oh hi, Mr. Monkwood isn't it? We visited you a couple of days ago didn't we, you're the clown guy?' Anthony responded, not really in the mood for a casual chat but aware of the inevitability now the story had broken completely.

'That's right' Monkwood said, laughing 'that sad clown, that's me. Anyway good idea getting the story out there like that, may give you some more leads, hopefully anyway' he said, still smiling.

'Well fingers crossed, although we've had a few the last day so we could be on the verge of a breakthrough anyway' Anthony lied.

Monkwood didn't believe that for one minute. He doubted very much they had a clue what was going on. Only the previous evening when he had called Bradfield to ask if he'd made his decision, the chief had grabbed the phone and asked him to release them both. It was hardly the behavior of a man on the verge of solving the case. Monkwood had hung up at that point, he'd had no need to speak to the Chief and there really was nothing he could do anyway.

'How's the mother in law?' Anthony asked him. The question threw Monkwood briefly; he'd momentarily forgotten that lie. 'Oh oh not good' he stammered over his response. 'Only a matter of time now, it's running out fast I think' he continued, suddenly wishing he'd not bothered to stop and talk to the Chief.

'Shame' Anthony said. 'Missing the wife and kid I expect?' he continued.

'More than you know' Monkwood replied, 'I just want them back if I'm honest, be glad when it's all over' he smiled again and then patted the chief on the back with the re-rolled newspaper. 'Anyway, good luck' Monkwood said, making his way out of the store.

Anthony watched him leave. He couldn't put his finger on why but he didn't like Monkwood, there was something about the man which bothered him. He guessed it was, more than likely that Monkwood was a clown and the chief's inordinate fear of them had probably clouded his judgment somewhat.

He paid for the newspaper and made his way back to the truck, he had no desire to read the story until he got himself back to the station. His fear of clowns was matched only by his fear of the press and their ability to manipulate. He hadn't disliked Henderson but he certainly hadn't trusted him either. As he arrived back at the station the Chief hoped Henderson had proven him wrong with the piece and more than that, he hoped the story would flush out some positive information or better still, encourage whoever was behind this to slip up before it was too late.

MOTHER & CHILD ABDUCTED IN EDGARTOWN

The quiet, sleepy Martha's Vineyard had a rude awakening this week in Edgartown. The ordinarily idyllic locale was harshly thrown into the twenty first century when two of its residents found themselves at the hands of a psychotic abductor.

Claire Bradfield (33) and her son Jake were mercilessly taken the day after young Jake's eighth birthday in a seemingly motiveless attack.

The whereabouts of Mrs. Bradfield and her young, helpless son are so far unknown.

The local chief of police, Anthony Leith, expressed his concern yesterday in a requested meeting with myself. Appealing for any witnesses to come forward, or anybody with any semblance of information, no matter how small, in regards to this 'monster'.

Whilst there are areas of the case which cause great concern, this reporter has been asked not to divulge all of the information in regards to the case.

'So far so good' thought Anthony. The story was at least out there and the public had been made aware and as requested, Henderson had kept his word and a lid on the details for now. Anthony read on.

What this reporter found most interesting about this case was the complete lack of preparation by the Edgartown Police Department. The basic methods of policing appear to have been overlooked and clearly the Chief of Police, whilst appearing to be an affable man, is completely out of his depth. With time being of the essence in this particular case and running out slowly, it does beg the question 'why not call in reinforcements?' Mrs. Bradfield and her son have been missing now for nearly three days. They could be at the hands of a rapist or pedophile and yet the Chief of Police had time to discuss the finer details of progressive rock music with me. Despite being a music aficionado, Anthony Leith or his deputy did not have the inclination to even make the local radio station aware of the missing mother and her child. We hope and pray that Claire and Jake Bradfield are returned safely to the loving arms of their broken husband and father James very soon. I fear, however, that as the clock ticks and they remain missing, with the Edgartown Police Department's best efforts not being nearly good enough, this story could have a bitter end.

Michael Henderson

Anthony threw the newspaper across the room, its pages scattered all over the floor in various angles. 'Fucking hack' he said under his breath, putting his head in his sweaty palms. It angered him greatly that Henderson had, whilst getting the story into the public consciousness, used it as an excuse to belittle the efforts of his colleagues and himself. In all honesty though, what angered him more was that Henderson was right. He'd seen through the façade of their ineptitude quickly and if he could, so would the abductor. Anthony looked at the clock. The time was now 10.17am. In just a matter of hours this could all be over, in one way or another.

Mickey Henderson sat at his desk eating a sugar coated, cholesterol filled donut, stopping occasionally to lick the grainy remnants of sucrose from the tips of his dirty fingers. Between each bite of carbohydrate he swigged coffee and puffed on a cigarette. The phones around the office were buzzing as usual and the other staff mulled around going about their daily routines. Henderson was due to go into town to interview a guy who had recently been released following a stint in the penitentiary for carjacking. Apparently he had some news about drugs being dealt inside by the wardens. Granted, it was nothing new but it was always good to do an expose and show people up. In fact Henderson had made his career out of making all kinds of seemingly decent people show up for the low life they were.

'MICKEY' shouted one of the men at the other end of the office 'GOT A CALL FOR YOU, SAYS ITS ABOUT THE EDGARTOWN PIECE.'

'Jesus another one' Henderson said 'I've had nothing but shit for brains crack pots all morning, this better not be another. That's the problem with these stories, always brings the freaks to the forefront. Stick it through Sam' Henderson finished his rant and waited for his phone to ring. For a man so untidy in appearance it was a wonder his desk was so well kept. A small filing tray to the left, an electronic typewriter in the middle, because he loved to do things the old fashioned way, and his phone to the right. Everything was all very neat and tidy. Not Mickey Henderson at all in fact, however, with his writing and with his job, he took those things deadly seriously. They were after all his lifeblood.

'Hello' he said, still finishing a mouthful of donut. 'Mr. Henderson, my name is Terrence Denton, you may have heard of me' the voice on the other phone said.

'Err, no, never have' Henderson said, already making his mind up in regards to the sanity levels of his caller. The man spoke again 'I'm a psychic medium, I have my own cable access show' Henderson thought for a moment and then the penny dropped, he did know this guy after all.

'Hang on one minute' he said 'I'm just going to put you on hold whilst I get a pen and paper' Henderson reached forward and pressed the mute button on the phone.

'HEY SAM' he shouted across the office 'IT'S THAT PSYCHIC MEDIUM GUY, THE ONE OFF THE TV, DENTON.' Sam laughed over the other side of the office, as did most of the men and women who'd heard. 'SORRY MICKEY,' Sam replied 'WAS ANOTHER FUCKING WACK JOB THEN' everybody including Henderson laughed. Once the office melee had died down he took the phone off mute.

'Sorry about that, can never find a pen when you need one can you?' Henderson lied 'so what can I do for you Mr. Denton?'

'It's a bit sketchy' Denton responded, oblivious to the fact the entire office around Henderson had been and still were making a mockery of him. 'I have been having this recurring dream about a woman and child trapped in a basement and their faces, their faces look very much like your picture of Mrs. Bradfield and her son.' Henderson was the last person to ever have an open mind about this type of thing. As far as he was concerned, it was nothing more than mumbo jumbo bullshit and he wasn't about to entertain this freak show's desire for cover time.

'Well that's a nice story, Mr. Denton, but what on earth does it say, other than you're having a bad dream and probably need to see a therapist' Henderson said in the most facetious manner he could.

'Very good, Mr. Henderson, I'm used to skepticism however' Denton replied, not at all perturbed by Henderson's change in attitude. 'I think he's going to kill them' Denton said. 'Yeah, well call the police then' Henderson said before hanging up. 'Hey guys' he said to nobody in particular 'stop putting these nut balls through to me, screen the calls for Christ sake I don't need to talk to every one of these weirdo's'

At that point one of the young girls came over to him and crouched down by his desk. Henderson was acutely aware of how her short skirt had ridden up to show the tops of her stockings. He doubted he could be less interested in whatever she had to say right now.

'I have a guy on the phone' she whispered, leaning in closer to him 'he said he knows exactly what is going on over in Edgartown and he knows who is involved'

'Really?' Henderson whispered back, keeping his sarcastic tone on a level, 'put him through then' Henderson watched as the young girl made her way back to her desk, her legs seeming to go on forever. As she put the call through Henderson made a conscious effort to make sure this would be the last one he took before he went out. He was already more than fed up with the crackpots who had been ringing in today and thoroughly regretted ever going to Edgartown to run the story in the first place. He picked the phone up again.

'Mr. Henderson' the voice spoke crisply and clearly on the other end before Henderson could even greet the caller. 'I have a lot of information which may be of use to you' Henderson laughed, outwardly so the caller could hear him.

'Yeah you and every caller today' he replied 'what you got that they haven't?'

'I know Mr. Bradfield had 72 hours to make a decision and if he hasn't made one by today, his wife and child will be dead' the man answered calmly and knowingly. Henderson paused, he was no longer laughing. He felt listening to this man he could have a genuine lead that may actually be relevant. Maybe now he'd get a shot at the Pulitzer he craved so much.

'Tell me everything you know' Henderson responded eagerly.

'Meet me in room 202, at the Marriot, in one hour and I will blow the lid on this whole thing Sir' said the man on the other end 'and come alone, this will be the story of your life' Henderson was skeptical and wary of meeting anybody he didn't know in a hotel room but this guy knew things and he needed to know exactly what.

'Why there, why not out in the open?' Henderson said, punting for a change in the venue.

'Because, Mr. Henderson, this story runs deeper than you could imagine and I am putting myself in grave danger just by talking to you' the man said 'meet me in an hour if you want to know

61

everything' At that the line went dead and Henderson felt dizzy with excitement. He had no idea what to expect but he knew one thing, he was about to get one hell of a story. He picked up his trench coat and made his way out of the office, talking to nobody as he left. He'd show the Edgartown Police how to solve a case and he'd be the hero of that little town. He wondered if they'd give him some kind of private getaway there. He really needed a break and where better to get one than the Vineyard.

Claire Bradfield and her son Jake sat silently in the partially lit Basement. Their captor had at least untied them and even put a TV in there. There was no television signal, of course, although he had the good grace to connect it to a DVD player. The only DVD provided, however, was a 3 hour kids TV special. It amused Jake and gave his infant brain something else to focus on. For Claire though, the fear of what could happen grew with every minute. She was progressing into cabin fever and could do nothing about it. It was time to try and fight, enough was enough. She wondered what the mad man had requested her husband do. All the clown had kept telling her was that James had a decision to make. What kind of decision left her and Jake trapped in a basement for three days? Claire felt angry with James, as though he somehow should have rescued them and been their knight in shining armor. How would he have known where to find them though? She really didn't know what to think anymore. She climbed the stairs and chanced the door handle again, knowing full well it would be locked. She'd thought about hiding somewhere when the clown next came but she knew there was nowhere to hide. He often held a gun and she couldn't risk putting her sons life in more danger when for all she knew the clown would let them go anyway. He hadn't hurt them in any way, had kept them fed and had to an extent seemed almost apologetic at times as if he wished he hadn't taken them. The worst part about the whole thing, other than the slop bucket they were being made to use as a toilet, was the not knowing whilst still having to remain strong for Jake. Claire was tired, they both were, she just wanted to go home.

She climbed back down the stairs and the glint of something caught by the light distracted her eye, nestling underneath the make shift travel bed the two of them had been sleeping on.

She bent down to pick up the object; it was a paperclip. In everyday life a common paperclip would be as relevant as dust on a desk, nothing at all but in this scenario, it offered an escape. How many films had Claire seen with her husband, which showed the ease of breaking and entering with a paperclip or some such object? Many, and although she knew the likelihood of that happening in the real world was small, a part of her felt it was time she had some luck. She climbed the stairs, straightening the paperclip with her fingers as she did. Jake oblivious as he watched the rolling children's programme on screen for an apparent limitless time.

Wiggling the straightened paperclip around in the lock Claire didn't really know what she was doing or whether she was doing it the right way but what the hell, she had nothing better to do other than sit and wait. She knew she would try this all day if she needed to, some hope was better than none at all.

Claire knew the clown was out as she'd heard the front door close and the now recognizable sound of his purring engine driving away. Just as a cat knows the sound of its owners car as it pulls up outside, she had also grown accustomed to her captors vehicle in the same way.

After twenty minutes she finally felt as though the clip was catching on something. She felt some give as she continued maneuvering. Whether it was psychological or not she couldn't say for sure but she definitely felt something and then suddenly 'NO' she cried, as she dropped the clip in the lock. It was gone. She peered through the hole and could just see, thanks to the light on the other side, the gleam of the pin laying in the lock chamber. Claire took the tip of her little finger and tried to ease the pin out but was just a painful fraction short of reaching it. Her frustration was overwhelming, she felt helpless, mortified as if her final chance of escape had eradicated completely. She looked over at Jake, his face blurred by the tears in her eyes. Due to her outburst he had finally distracted himself from the TV screen.

'What's the matter mummy?' he asked, concerned before leaving the chair and climbing to the top of the stairs with her. This was the first time she had cried since they were taken, in front of him at least. She'd cried plenty when he was asleep, enough to fill the slop bucket twice over. Claire held Jakes hand softly 'Nothing honey' she lied

'Mummy just gets a bit frustrated sometimes, I want to go home now' she said, stroking his fingers.

'So do I' Jake answered, starting to get upset 'I miss daddy and it's scary down here. I don't like clowns anymore' he said the last part as a kind of afterthought and it made Claire smile through her tears. 'neither do I' she answered. It dawned on her at that point how small Jakes hands were by comparison to her own.

'OK we're going to try something' she said 'see in there' gesturing towards the lock 'I dropped a pin, can you see if you can get it out for me?' He peered into the hole and then put his finger in the lock, easily pulling the paperclip out and giving it to her.

'Yes!' Claire exclaimed, kissing Jake on the head. 'you can go back and watch your programme now' she said and off he went, back to the chair.

Once again Claire spent the next half an hour vainly fiddling the clip in the lock, only this time being extra careful not to drop it again. Just as she was about to give up she heard a 'CLICK'

'Surely not' she said to herself. Reaching forward, her hand trembling with a mixture of fear and anticipation, she placed her hand on the cold metal handle and pulled. The door clicked, and then creaked open, bathing the entire basement in light from the windows in the hallway. Claire felt total euphoria. They were fee.

'Jake' she called down to him. He looked up at her and smiled. 'We're going home?'

'Yes darling, we're going home' she said. Jake ran up the steps and joined her at the top. Claire made her way down the hallway, tightly gripping Jakes hand as she did. She didn't remember how she'd got here, only that something had been put over her face and she woke up in the basement. She was surprised at how homely the house appeared, it was actually nice and nothing like she had expected. Not that she had expected much. She looked into the front room, and there were pictures of the man who had taken them, the clown, with a child and woman. Claire couldn't imagine this monster being anything close to a family man. She was still holding Jakes hand as the Clown came out of the kitchen and punched her full in the face, she didn't even see him. She was still holding Jakes hand as she passed out cold, as Jake screamed for his mum. In her eagerness to get out, to get that door open, to escape, Claire hadn't heard the car come back and she hadn't realized the man had arrived home. Oh but he had heard her, he had heard her trying to get out, so he waited and then pounced out of the door, like a fully living jack in the box. Surprise!

Mickey Henderson knocked on the door of room 202 at The Marriot Hotel across town, two minutes shy of the hour. He heard the door click as the inhabitant opened it. Standing there was a tall smartly dressed man, in his early forties. With slicked back jet black hair and wearing a pin stripe suit he looked as though he had wandered straight off Wall Street. Mickey held out his hand but the man did not shake it, instead, he waved Henderson through and pointed towards one of two chairs sitting opposite each other.

'Can I get you a drink, Mr. Henderson' the man asked, closing the door, before making his way over to the mini bar.

'A soda water would be good,' Henderson lied. The man turned around and smiled at him, 'With or without the scotch?' he enquired craftily. Henderson thought for a minute.

'Yeah go on then, you only live once,' Henderson replied.

'You're damn right' the man said laughing. 'Live a lot, not a little,' he added. He quickly mixed the drink, making one for himself and sat down opposite Henderson, passing him the drink on the way.

'So, are you going to give me your name now?' Henderson asked the man.

'Right now my name is not important,' the man replied, however, what I am about to tell you is, greatly and you have to ensure you get this all down,' the man replied, taking a sip of his drink at the exact same time Henderson did the same.

'How can I report on this if I don't have a credible source?' Henderson asked, digging for some kind of confirmation of the man's name. The man smiled.

'After I tell you what I am about to, I can assure you, no source will be necessary.'

Henderson nodded his head in understanding. 'OK, I'll switch this on,' Henderson said, putting the Dictaphone on record.

The man nodded his head and downed the rest of his drink in one before placing the glass on the floor, to the side of the chair he was sitting on.

'Your kidnapper's name is Mr. Barry Monkwood, lives over in Edgartown, plies his trade there as a clown, believe it or not,' the man said, laughing at the last part of his statement. 'Does kids parties of all things.'

Henderson raised his eyebrows. 'How the hell do you know all of this?' he asked skeptically.

'Patience, Mr. Henderson, a good story has to build you'll agree, we will get to that part' the man replied, running his hand through his slicked back hair as he did.

'Mr. Monkwood has been given two people from the same family to abduct and give whichever family member he's left behind 72 hours to choose which one to kill and then Mr. Monkwood has to kill one and return the other, or leave them somewhere to be found safely' the man continued. Henderson didn't say anything, he began to feel hot and his neck and back were perspiring. It was a blazing day out there again and this hotel lacked the necessity of an air conditioning unit. 'Or, of course, he will have to kill them both if no decision is made, either way, someone dies' the man said, quite coldly.

'I need to call the Edgartown PD and get them over to this guy's house right away' Henderson said, reaching into his pocket for the phone. The man put the flat of his hand up.

'No, not yet, there's still plenty of time, nothing will happen before six' he said, still holding his hand up.

'But how do you know all of this, who is making this guy do this and why? Has this Monkwood told you?' Henderson replied, removing his hand from his pocket, the phone still in its place.

'No, no I've never met him before, the person who told me is the same person who is making Mr. Monkwood do this' the man answered 'you see, poor Mr. Monkwood has no choice' Henderson didn't understand, the situation seemed instantly more complicated than it had been only five minutes ago.

'This makes no sense to me at all' Henderson said. The man smiled again.

'It won't I'm afraid' he responded 'Mr. Monkwood's wife and daughter were abducted and he had 72 hours to choose which one to save' the man continued, watching as Henderson's mouth dropped. 'Naturally, he chose his daughter to save because, well to be honest, who wouldn't choose his own child in the end?' he continued. Henderson felt as cold as he had hot earlier and a shiver ran down the length of his spine, causing the hair on the back of his neck to stand on end.

'The problem is, as with every good game, there is always some kind of hidden clause and in his case, although he chose to save his daughter, to get her back, he had to start the next leg of the game, by choosing the next target. Tonight someone will die Mr. Henderson, that's a guarantee and as a result of that, Mr. Monkwood should get his daughter back' the man finished, smiling at Henderson.

'But why, why would anybody tell you all of this?' Henderson asked, no longer concerned about the story as much as he was the reason behind it.

'How do you feel, right now, Mr. Henderson?' the man asked, not answering the question at all.

'Shocked I guess, I don't think anybody realizes what is involved here' Henderson responded.

'No, no Mr. Henderson, you misunderstand me, how do YOU feel, in yourself, right now?' the man asked again, staring intently into Henderson's eyes.

Henderson realized he felt warm again but also nauseas, he went to stand up but couldn't move. His arms, his legs, the whole body was completely immoveable, as though a heavy weight was pushing down on him. In his head Henderson wanted to ask what was happening but his mouth suddenly wouldn't work, apart from his eyes, his whole body had shut down.

'By now you're wondering what is happening to you, Mr. Henderson,' the man said, clasping his hands together and leaning forward in the chair. 'I slipped a neuromuscular blocking agent in your drink, Mr. Henderson. It's fast acting, you didn't feel anything' he continued. 'You see, I have a problem, not with you I hasten to add, but a problem all the same' The man stood up and walked over to his briefcase and placed it down on the single bed in the room. Flipping open the clasps he pulled something out and closed it again. Clutching a newspaper he held it up in front of Henderson so he could see it.

'Two years ago in Florida my wife and daughter were taken from me by a man who gave me just 72 hours to decide which of them he should murder.' The man sat down again. 'I went to the press and the police and of course nobody could do anything. There was no motive, no rhyme nor reason and nothing linking them with the person who had them.' The man stopped, thinking, while the comatose yet conscious Henderson looked on.' The press dubbed him "The Choice Maker" and ultimately I was left with the decision of choosing one or calling his bluff. I chose the latter,' the man said, clasping his hands together again and leaning forward in the chair. 'I never saw my wife and daughter again and nobody was ever caught, Mr. Henderson. The story became the following day's trash and eventually it was forgotten about. For a while, of course, the police hounded me, thought I had something to do with it and absolutely I didn't. I've spent the last two years trying to find out something, anything, that may lead me to discovering who took them and why,' he stopped again, looking at the floor and then looked up, intently into Henderson's eyes. 'Which leads me to you,' the man spoke softly, clasping his hands together tightly. 'Two nights ago my phone rang and on the other end was a voice I recognized, a voice from two years previously, and he told me something I never expected to hear. He told me my daughter was still alive, not my wife, God rest her. The man told me I had an option to get her back and he would tell me how that could be made so.' The man got up from the chair and made his way to the mini bar to pour another drink. He looked back at Henderson. 'Sorry, no point doing one for you,' he said, before making his way back to the chair with the drink and sitting down again. 'He said I hadn't understood the rules of the game before and he had decided to give me a chance. Naturally I didn't believe him, why should I? Then he let me speak to her on the phone. I spoke to my daughter, Mr. Henderson. I heard her voice. He went on to tell me everything I have told you today about Mr. Monkwood and Mrs. Bradfield and her son, warning me that if I went to the police then my daughter would be killed, no more chances.' The man put his glass down on the floor. 'Which is why I couldn't risk giving you my name while you were in a position to use it,' he said. 'So now we're here, you sitting there, me sitting here and you wondering what any of this really has to do with you. Well nothing, to be honest with you, but the voice on the phone, the 'choice maker' if you like, has brought you into his game.' The man rose from the chair again and made his way back to the briefcase, still laying on the bed, opening it. Taking something else out he made his way back to the chair, screwing a silencer on the end of the gun he was now holding as he did. Sitting down he pointed the gun at Henderson's head. Henderson didn't react, although the man was sure a slight flicker was apparent in his eyes. Inwardly, Henderson was petrified, if his muscles would allow him to he'd have been sick right there. He was completely paralyzed by the drug he had been given and by fear. Henderson could hear his heart pounding in his ear drums, could even feel the blood surging through his veins but he could not move even a finger.

'I think The Choice Maker is annoyed about your story, or the fact attention has been drawn to that little town before he's had a chance to finish playing out his game,' the man said, 'and I'm very sorry, Mr. Henderson, I really am, but unless I do this, unless I kill you, right now, I will never see my daughter again. I cannot risk losing her for a second time.' The man's index finger squeezed harder on the trigger of the gun aimed at Henderson's head. With a delicate pop the gun exploded its contents and the back of the wall behind Henderson was immediately smothered in blood, shaped like the plume of a peacock's feathers. Henderson's expression didn't change. He remained seated in the chair, blood dripping from the hole in the front of his forehead, his lifeless eyes staring blankly in the same direction they had been before. The man rose from his position, put the gun back in the briefcase and made his way out of the hotel room. Henderson's corpse sat alone in the chair, the only sound coming from the room was the faint whirring of the Dictaphone recording in his pocket.

The Chief, Jennifer, Jed and Eric Blane sat in the front room of James Bradfield's home just before 5.50pm that evening. The kidnappers call had been anticipated all day and the reasonably luke warm response to Henderson's article had left them with no further leads. Anthony had discussed in depth with James exactly what to say to the kidnapper, there was no way in hell he intended to make any choice and Anthony told him to stick to his guns. Bradfield had convinced himself that there was no way this man would carry out his threat and the police officers felt the same. Without a motive, what was the point?

'OK you're sure you are happy to do this?' Anthony checked with Bradfield for probably the tenth time in the last hour. 'I'm not letting this bastard take control' Bradfield said. The four police officers had watched James Bradfield turn from a wreck into a man willing to fight in the past few days. Eric Blanes original reservations were no longer in existence, he had grown a great amount of respect for Bradfield. They all had.

At exactly 6pm the phone did, as expected ring. Bradfield answered it with steely determination. 'Hello' he said, sternly and confidently.

'Your decision please, Mr. Bradfield' the voice said on the other end. James felt exhausted, mentally and emotionally but he knew Claire and Jake were feeling much worse.

'Let me speak to them?' James replied. There was a short pause as the man on the other end of the phone considered the request.

'No, make a decision, Mr. Bradfield' the voice on the other end of the phone replied, unwilling to entertain the request.

'How do I know they are alive, how do I know you even have them?' Bradfield asked.

'Because, Mr. Bradfield if I don't have them, then where are they?' the man calmly responded. 'Make a choice, Mr. Bradfield, or I will do it for you' he continued, forcefully and threateningly ending his sentence.

'I will not, I WILL NOT choose,' Bradfield said, shouting the words the second time. Again there was a pause before the man finally responded.

'Hickory dickory dock, the mouse ran up the clock, the clock struck seven and *they* went to heaven, hickory dickory dock.' suddenly the line went dead. Bradfield stood there holding the phone to his ear, saying nothing and hearing nothing on the other end of the line. Anthony walked over to him and took the phone from his hand, before listening to the receiver himself.

'What did he say?' Anthony asked Bradfield, putting his hand on his shoulder.

'He didn't' was all Bradfield replied, before slowly walking back into the living room.

'I think it's time we involved the Massachusetts PD' Eric said. 'This could go on and we're in this above our heads' At that,

Bradfield snapped, kicking the small coffee table in the front room over.

'Oh now you're in this over your fucking heads are you?!' he said sarcastically to Blane 'you lot haven't done anything, you've been no use, what's the point of involving *real* police now the time has run out?' Bradfield continued.

The last comment niggled Anthony, it got to them all in fact. What with Henderson's article and Bradfields opinions today had resulted in a lot of home truths. Anthony felt gut wrenchingly sick. They had, despite their best efforts, failed Bradfield. The four police officers and James Bradfield stood in the middle of the front room, nobody saying a word for some time. None of them knew what to do. Would the man call again, would he finally reveal what he wanted? Maybe there was a motive that hadn't been revealed. Maybe, maybe, maybe but in all, it was just ifs and buts.

At 7pm the phone rang again. Anthony went over to pick it up 'it's probably Henderson' he said, 'he said he'd call to find out what, if anything happened, to continue the report' 'Yeah well give him a piece of our mind please' Jenny said. Anthony picked up the phone 'Bradfield Residence' he said 'Chief Anthony Leith speaking'

'Why hello chief' it was the man again 'no time to waste is there, although clearly there is, you haven't done a great deal with yours have you?' the man said, clearly enjoying himself by the tone of his voice.

'What have you done with Mrs. Bradfield and her son?' Anthony demanded to know.

'How many of you are there Chief?' the man answered the question with one of his own.

'There are five of us, why?' Anthony asked, his patience stretched at the tone of the man's voice. His quiet, understated style of speaking was chilling and Anthony felt his spine stiffen with tension.

'Can you see the memorial bridge from there?' the man asked.

'Yes you know we can' Anthony answered, hissing through his teeth as he tried to stifle his rage. The man laughed.

'Yes, yes I do don't I?' he replied 'well better get down there then and quick, it'll take the five of you to pick up the pieces' the man said, real vitriol echoing in his voice as he spat the words out. Again the line went dead.

Everybody in the room watched the blood run from Anthony's face.

'Oh God what did he say?' Bradfield asked as he began to bite furiously on his bottom lip. Anthony regained his composure.

'OK he wants us to go down to the Memorial Bridge, it's probably another part of his ridiculous game' Anthony said to them all. He looked at James 'You stay here' James shook his head.

'Absolutely not, I am coming as well, whatever it is, I am coming as well' he said. The words did not come out easily, the saliva in his mouth had all but disappeared, he felt empty inside, as though he was running on autopilot. He knew without any doubt though, he had to go.

The four police officers and James Bradfield made their way down to the pond and the Memorial Bridge. It wasn't easy to get there by vehicle so they decided to walk the short five minute journey across the beach.

The night air was warm and sticky. Now it felt as though the storm was coming for sure.

On arrival none of them could see anything of relevance. The waves lapped the shoreline as they always did and light generated by the moon flickered off them reflecting onto the sand, making it appear white.

'What does he want us here for?' Bradfield asked, looking around for an answer.

Nobody spoke, they were all so busy looking for some idea as to why they were there. The silence was interrupted by the sounds of the Chief's phone ringing.

'Chief Anthony Leith' he said as he answered the phone.

'How many of you went down to the bridge Chief?' the man asked, taking Anthony by surprise.

'All of us' he replied 'what the fuck do you want us to do?' the chief's anger was boiling over, for all to hear.

'All of you?' the man asked, as if questioning Anthony 'well you can see Mr. Bradfield's house from there, does that look like all of you went?' he said cryptically, laughing at the same time.

Anthony looked back at the house in the distance and could clearly see the figure of somebody standing in the window of the attic of Bradfield's house, its light still on. The figure was doing something, but Anthony couldn't make out what it was. He walked a little further forward trying to adjust his eyes, the other four watching him as he moved.

'What are you looking at?' Bradfield asked as Antony suddenly realized.

'He's waving, the fucker is waving at us' Anthony started to run, oblivious to whether the man was still on the phone or not. Jenny, Eric and Bradfield swiftly followed. The sand felt heavy under their feet and the ability to run at speed was practically impossible. As they moved across the hindering grains beneath them Jed, still in the distance, noticed a vehicle moving at high speed down the road in the opposite direction of the Bradfield's residence.

'WAIT' Jed shouted at them all ahead of him. Bradfield stopped but the police officers ahead continued in the direction of the house. 'There's only one road to and from your house?' Jed asked. Bradfield nodded his head in agreement. Jed took flight, up the bank and towards the road where his and Eric's patrol car was parked. He flung the door open and jumped in, screeching off down the road in pursuit of the car he'd just seen pass him only moments before. Bradfield continued to stand on the beach, watching from where he'd stopped.

Anthony was the first up the stairs of the Bradfield's home, swiftly followed by Jenny. Eric Blane was still negotiating the steps leading up to Bradfield's front porch but had done well, considering his girth, to even make it this far.

The steps to the attic were still down; nestled on the landing floor and the light above remained on. Anthony looked up into the bright room above, immediately aware of his own mortality. A sense of self-preservation washed over him as he considered taking the first step. He had seen someone less than a couple of minutes previously, waving from the attic window. The top of his head tingled with each increasing climb towards the opening of the attic. His head it seemed was all too aware that somebody could be waiting up there with a pick axe to impale straight through the top of his skull. Anthony sensed danger but as his forehead finally eclipsed the opening of the

73

attic and his eyes came into sight, it took only an instant for his brain to register what his eyes were seeing. Anthony uttered a low, guttural 'NO' as his mouth filled with vomit and his hands lost their grip on the attic opening. Falling down the steps in a hail of sweat and sick Anthony crashed to the ground in front of Jenny's feet. Jenny couldn't comprehend what she was witnessing. Her natural instinct told her that someone out of sight had attacked Anthony but that was obviously not the case. As she tried to register what was happening Bradfield brushed past her and began to climb the steps with wild abandonment, not in the least fearful for this own safety.

Anthony lamely reached out a hand to try and grab Bradfield's foot and stop him, but it was an effortless gesture. All the Chief, Jenny or Eric Blane could do was listen to the high pitched hysterical screams as Bradfield saw the decapitated heads of his wife and child laying on the attic floor. Scrawled in blood on the back wall were the words 'This was your choice'. Bradfield collapsed to his knees, silently screaming at the floor, his head between his hands.

Jed raced down the road at nearly 100mph and he could see the lights ahead of the car which had recently passed him on its way from Bradfield's house. He closed in on the car which was clearly unable to reach the kinds of speeds he could. The adrenaline raced through his veins, he badly wanted to be the hero, needed to be. Before he could think he was on the tail of the brown Datsun ahead and he found himself deliberating the consequences of hitting the car in the rear. This wasn't a movie, he may not necessarily just run it off the road, he could himself be involved in a terrible accident. The other thought bearing down on Jed was the possibility this may not be anything to do with the Bradfield case and he was about to run an innocent bystander off the road.

'Fuck it' Jed muttered to himself 'innocent bystanders don't drive like this guy is' and at that Jed forced his foot down on the accelerator, pressing the pedal to the floor. The police car careered into the back of the Datsun, sending it spinning off the road, clipping a telegraph pole on its way. The force of the collision matched with the speed the car was travelling sent it up on its side as it slid through the undergrowth off the road, grinding to a halt, the wheels off the ground still spinning furiously.

Jed span his car to a half with a violent skid. In fact, little had been made of the impact on his car, it had been like the movies after all. Jed jumped out of his vehicle and ran to the Datsun on its side. Pulling his gun out from its holster, Jed threw the passenger door open. Looking down into the driver's side Jed saw, wedged up against the window, a man, dressed as a clown. The clown, with it's sad, painted on upside down smile looked at Jed, and put his hands over his face, as if to protect himself from the possibility of a gun shot.

'Please, please don't kill me' he begged, peering at Jed through his fingers. 'HE MADE ME DO IT' he screamed with so much anger, a shiver ran down Jed's spine. He pointed his gun to one side and looked down at the trapped clown pinned in the car.

'You have the right to remain silent' he said. Those words brought instant relief. Jed finally felt as though the nightmare was over.

Chapter Nine

Barry Monkwood sat in the small five by nine cell staring at the wall. The blood of Claire and Jake Bradfield had dried on his outfit and hands. He was still dressed as the clown, making him appear to be insane. He wasn't though, not really.

Monkwood sat their staring, trying to block the thoughts from his mind but the more he tried the more in vain it was. He could see himself pull the trigger, he could see Jake and Claire's bodies lying lifeless on the ground and he could hear the voice telling him to 'chop off their heads'. As hard as he willed himself to think of no more, he could see himself doing it, oh and the blood, so much blood. Monkwood sat there, tears streaming down his face, his make-up smudged by them. His left shoulder hurt from the accident but the police were not interested. He figured he had no right to expect them to be and they had every right to make him suffer, he'd done a terrible thing. He needed to tell them why, but that wasn't the deal, the voice had been very specific. 'Your wife and child will be returned if you do this, if you take the rap they will be returned to you' He had no reason to trust the voice but he had every reason to put hope in it's honesty because that was all he had left. Barry just wanted his family back and maybe once they returned the truth would come out anyway, they wouldn't let him suffer in silence. What if they were not returned though, what if they never came back, then what? The voice had said they would return within 72 hours of his task completing. He had spoken to them both on the phone and he knew they were alive. Monkwood realized that three more days of this, three more days of being vilified by the police and probably the press as well would be worth it if the ultimate goal was realized, the return of his family.

Barry was scared though, petrified. Oh he'd done a terrible thing an awful, evil, terrible thing and he would never be able to live with that. He hoped his wife could and his daughter, hoped they would realize that everything he had done had all been for them.

Barry Monkwood had like many of the residents, grown up in Edgartown, he knew his life there was over, whatever happened from there on in. Monkwood was set to be the most hated man in Martha's Vineyard, an out and out pariah. He just prayed they would all understand, that the whole town would put itself in his shoes and see what they would have done.

'You should have just gone to the Police?' they will say. Of course, that would have been easy but the voice had been clear. 'Go to the Police' and your wife and child are dead. 'Fine, then make a mistake, let the police find them without implicating yourself, do something, anything' Again a fine suggestion but the outcome of that was always going to be the same. As the voice had said 'Anything goes wrong and the game is not carried out exactly as I instruct, then your wife and child will die'

Monkwood had no option. The Choice Maker had chosen the Bradfields as victims but why Monkwood didn't know. Fate had drawn him to the Bradfield's for the party he was sure. He'd been there that day knowing full well he had to abduct Mrs. Bradfield the following day. It was as though events had come together to ensure he'd be there. The Bradfields home was slightly secluded and only had one road in and out, he figured he could easily abduct Mrs. Bradfield and her Son, but how?

In the end sabotaging the car and then being conveniently on hand to offer Claire a lift while she was walking became the most obvious solution. She'd met him the day before at her Sons party, she knew who Barry Monkwood was anyway, she'd seen him around town. What was there to be cautious of? Everybody in Edgartown was so nice, so caring and so trustworthy. Offering her the lift into town was too simple and her and Jake the ride home even easier. Conveniently passing once again, on his way back from town, just as Jake was creating about having to walk home and easy does it, Mrs. Bradfield and her son are in the car. Now three days on Barry Monkwood sat in the cell, sat there feeling sick to the stomach and devoid of all spirit. He'd been made to do a terrible thing. He began crying again, sobbing uncontrollably. Why had the man chosen him in the first place, why his wife and child? Barry didn't understand, didn't even know if there was a motive, he just understood that within a few days everything had changed for so many people.

Chief Anthony Leith looked through the viewing door of the cell and glared at the clown, sitting there crying, its make-up running.

'I've always hated Clowns' he said to nobody in particular under his breath 'and now I know why' Anthony kicked the cell door in sheer frustration, causing the clown to jump and look up. Anthony continued to glare at him for a few moments more without breaking eye contact, before moving away.

'Chief there's someone here to see you' Jenny said from behind her cramped desk, as she typed up some notes. 'Detectives Ashworth and Rosemount from the Massachusetts Police Department' she continued.

A tall, red haired, stocky man, probably in his late thirties stood with a much smaller, petit woman with long dark hair and darker eyes. She appeared to be in her early twenties and Anthony was momentarily taken aback by how strikingly beautiful she was.

'How can I help?' he said, offering his hand to the man, who shook it firmly, almost breaking Anthony's fingers in the process.

'I'm Detective Ashworth, this is Detective Rosemount' the man answered 'we're taking over this case and moving your prisoner off the island and back to state' he continued.

'You can't do that, he's our prisoner' Anthony protested. Jenny stopped what she was doing and looked up from the paperwork.

'I'm afraid we can Sir' Detective Rosemount said firmly and sternly, immediately blowing away her previous complexion. She no longer appeared to be as breathtakingly beautiful as Anthony first perceived. She now gave off the persona of a school mistress. 'We have a missing person reported in Massachusetts' she continued 'the reporter, Michael Henderson, who was here yesterday' she said, raising her eyebrows at Anthony in an almost accusational gesture.

'Didn't do you any justice there did he Chief?' Detective Ashworth said with an arrogant tone to his voice.

'I fail to see the relevance?' Anthony answered, tired of the detectives, tired of the case, tired of life. In his head Anthony told himself not to be so stubborn, let them take Monkwood over to their station, he could wash his hands of the whole thing and get back to trying to rebuild the towns faith in the Department. They had at least caught the man, or Jed had.

'The relevance Chief' the man said again, condescendingly 'is that Henderson is an on call guy, he never makes himself unavailable, he will work 24/7 if necessary and now, since he went out earlier yesterday, the guy isn't even answering his phone' the detective scratched his chin, as if thinking of a grandiose way to finish his minor speech.

'We think your guy in there knows something' Detective Rosemount said, gesturing towards the cell 'and we are taking him' she finished, pulling out the necessary transfer papers.

'All signed by Judge Deeds' Detective Ashworth said. There was nothing Anthony could do, he had to suck it up and deal with it. Monkwood was going across the water and nobody was going to be able to stop that. It felt like a real kick in the teeth. They'd done the hard part and now the city big shots were going to take the glory. It didn't feel that way to Jenny though, she felt it was retribution for the mess they'd made of the investigation and she was no doubt right. She had taken James Bradfield to the hospital and left him there, sedated and in the capable hands of the doctors and nurses. She knew however, that Bradfield would never be the same man. They had failed him.

Antony opened the cell door and the expressionless clown gazed up at him from his position slouched in the corner.

'Time to go, they're taking you to the City' Anthony said, feeling nothing but complete hatred for what sat before him.

'East Falmouth, to be precise' Ashworth interrupted.

Barry Monkwood slowly climbed to a standing position and feet scuffing the floor made his way out of the cell. The effort it took him was clearly apparent, as if heavy weights the size of cars sat on each shoulder.

The two detectives led Monkwood out of the station and down to their car, with Jenny and Anthony watching from the window. Neither of them said anything as the car pulled away, making the short journey towards the ferry crossing.

As the rear lights dimmed in the distance, Anthony reached out for his keys and grabbed them from his desk. Jenny placed her hand on his arm.

'We did what we could' she said to him, papering over the cracks in an attempt to make him and indeed herself feel better. Anthony reached his hand up and placed it over hers.

'You and I both know that isn't true Jen' he said, not looking at her 'and I'm going home' With that Anthony opened the door and made his way out of the office. Just four nights ago Anthony had been sitting in this very room willing something interesting to happen in Edgartown. Now it had he harked after his previous boring existence, because although it had been predictable, it had at least been safe. Anthony climbed in his car, craving a comfort zone long since gone.

Less than an hour later as Anthony Leith sat in his armchair reflecting on events Detectives Ashworth and Rosemount arrived back at the East Falmouth Police station. For the entire journey Barry Monkwood had said nothing and neither Detective had said a word to him.

Barry Monkwood was signed in at the desk and they led him through to the interview room and sat him down.

'Do you want a drink?' Rosemount asked him 'A coffee perhaps?' as she slid the chair out at the small table and sat opposite him. Monkwood shook his head. He wanted nothing.

Ashworth stood in the corner, casting an eye over the clown.

'Why'd you do it?' he asked suddenly, taking a match from the box in his pocket and placing the end of it in his mouth to chew on. 'Why kidnap an innocent woman and her son for no apparent reason and do what you did?' Monkwood said nothing, he just sat there staring at the walls.

'You were fucking her right?' Ashworth asked nonchalantly. 'That's it isn't it? You were fucking her and then she wouldn't leave her husband for you and you flipped,' Ashworth continued, not believing one word of what he was saying but trying all the same to gauge a flicker of a reaction. There was nothing.

'I want a Lawyer' Monkwood finally spoke, his voice cracked and croaky due to the length of time he had been sitting in silence.

'We'll call your Lawyer' Rosemount replied. Monkwood shook his head.

'I don't have a Lawyer, you need to provide me with one' Monkwood said, his voice returning to its normal level.

'Who doesn't have a Lawyer nowadays?' Ashworth said, still chewing furiously on his match.

'I never needed one before' Monkwood responded; now making eye contact with Ashworth.

'We can bring a state one in' Rosemount said, 'but it'll be tomorrow now'

Monkwood nodded his head in understanding.

'Fine, but I won't be talking until then, I am not saying anything to anybody until I have a Lawyer' Monkwood responded.

'No problem' Ashworth said, picking the splintered match from his mouth and flicking it on the floor 'we'll get you in a cell, get this shit cleaned off you, get you in a nice uniform and get you some representation tomorrow' Ashworth made his way over to Monkwood and leaned over him, his hands on the table. 'We're dying to know what's been going on in your fucked up head'

Juanita Gonzalez made her way to the cupboard where all of the cleaning products were kept. Her trolley sat where she had left it the day before and everything was in its right place.

Generally most people wouldn't acquire a great amount of joy from cleaning but Juanita loved it. She'd worked for the Marriot hotel for nearly fifteen years and they loved her too. She'd seen five managers come and go and had the greatest respect for all of them. She was one of the Marriot family and not seen as a downtrodden cleaner. The Marriot looked after their staff, whatever level they were at. Making her way down the corridors Juanita spent the next hour and a half giving all of the rooms due new occupancy an express clean. This meant a quick going over of the surfaces, the bathroom and a change of bedding and away we go, the room was ready for that day's occupant.

In most cases, the visitors to the Marriot were really only attending for a day or two at a time, either on business or some kind of illicit meeting. Rarely did any of the people there stay longer, apart from the man in room 202. That room had been booked out for nearly two weeks and for that time Juanita hadn't once seen a single person enter or leave. Oddly though, the room had always looked occupied in that time, despite the lack of presence.

Juanita used her pass card to make her way into the room. The man sitting in the room, staring at the door, took her aback. After all this time she hadn't actually expected someone to be there. She briefly considered speaking before her brain registered what her eyes were looking at. The man, a neat, round hole in his forehead sat there, mouth open, his skin waxy and pallid. A spew of bloody mess splattered all over the wall behind him, darkened where it had long since dried. Most people would react the same in such a situation and bolt out of the room but not Juanita. She had been raised in a rough neighborhood and seen more than anyone's fair share of bodies in her time, thanks to the gang culture she was immersed in as a youth.

She walked over to the body and realized the man had a familiar face, she had seen him before, she was sure. Juanita checked and doubled checked, looking at the man's face to make sure he was definitely real and this wasn't some awful practical joke. The grey blandness of his skin made him appear somewhat wax like. Juanita was certain this was a dead body. She knew he hadn't been there long, less than twenty four hours, because it was around this time the previous day she'd cleaned the room and there had definitely been no body to clean around then.

For the first time since she'd walked in the room Juanita felt a sudden pang of fear and concern. Ever since she'd entered and laid eyes on the dead body, she'd assumed this man had killed himself.

Looking around, Juanita realized there was no gun, no weapon of any kind.

Careful not to touch anything, Juanita backed out of the room, conscious of the fact this was apparently a murder scene. Putting on her rubber cleaning gloves, she pulled the door closed, aware that she had already touched the handle and the door with her bare hands on the way in.

Juanita was now more concerned than ever before. She realized the Police would want to take her prints to rule her out and then what would they find? No doubt the record she already had for theft and burglary. OK those were things she'd done twenty five years before but if her employers found out, then how understanding and thoughtful would the Marriot be? It didn't matter that for fifteen years there had never been a single complaint about her, mud sticks and Juanita knew it. Pondering what to do about the body in room 202, Juanita made her way down the corridor, the squeaky wheel on her trolley announcing her arrival long before she got there.

Billy Preston was twenty three, a shy way off twenty four. His mum had been a big fan of the singer Billy Preston so it stood to reason he'd get that name, given that he already had the surname in place ready. It was said that Billy's Mum, Claudette, had been such a fan of Billy Preston, she'd even married a man with the surname for the very purpose.

Billy would never know the answer to that for sure, his parents had been killed in a car accident when he was just five years of age. He had vague, though not overwhelming recollections of his parents, but most of what he knew came from his Aunt Sheila. Billy's Mum's sister had raised him after his parents had passed and raised him well.

He was very nearly a fully-fledged lawyer, his firm making his services available to the local Massachusetts Police Department by way of training him for free. It was good work experience if nothing else and Billy had taken part in some interesting cases, albeit only two. In both cases he had defended his client well and had got the last off on a slight misdemeanor. Billy enjoyed the fight and enjoyed winning, two combinations perfect for a successful career in law.

Billy sat in the reception area of the Massachusetts Police Department. He had been here before and found the Male detective, whose name he couldn't recall, dislikeable and standoffish. The woman, he seemed to recall her name was Rosemount was less of a pain. It was Detective Rosemount who met him. She introduced herself and led Preston down the short corridor to the cells, briefly explaining what the alleged criminal had done. He had to admit, it sounded cut and dried already.

Detective Rosemount opened the door to cell number 3 and led Billy in. A small, disheveled man sat hunched in the corner, looking down between his knees, as if he were some overgrown, recently scolded child.

'Mr. Monkwood' Detective Rosemount said, breaking the silence 'This is Mr. Preston, he's here to counsel you' Barry Monkwood looked up and stared blankly at Billy Preston, he was surprised how young the lawyer looked, practically a teenager. Monkwood stared down at the floor. Rosemount pointed to a red button on the wall by the door. 'You want to go hit this button, any problems at all in fact, hit the button' she said to Graham, gesturing and at that, turned and exited the cell, closing the door behind her. The room was completely white with white walls, white ceilings, a white bed, a white porcelain sink and a white porcelain toilet. Billy decided the surroundings were more reminiscent of an archetypal mental ward than a prison. He sat on the edge of the bed.

'Mr. Monkwood I'm here to counsel you' Billy said, staring intently at the man hunched in the corner. Barry Monkwood sat silently for a moment and then looked at Billy for an unnerving amount of time.

'You're very young' he said, biting on his index finger as he did 'what do you think you can do to help me?' Billy pondered the question for a moment.

'Perhaps if you tell me the story, tell me what happened and why, I can help you' Billy answered 'What you say to me stays with me, I'm like your Doctor, nothing gets repeated, it is strictly confidential information until such a time that it needs to be otherwise' This seemed to alert Monkwood and his eyes widened, he suddenly looked much more interested than he had thus far.

'When would such a time arise, Mr. Preston, such a time that what I tell you is no longer confidential?' Monkwood asked him.

Billy was intrigued, this man didn't seem crazy, he had the eyes of a man haunted but not a man who had lost his mind. Billy had seen men who had lost their minds before and this was not one of them. He needed to know what Monkwood had to tell him, not just because it was his job, he wanted to understand his client.

'If we go to trial' Billy answered 'then it is no longer confidential information but a case of public record' Monkwood laughed 'If we go to trial, Mr. Preston?' he said smiling 'I don't think there is any doubt this will go to trial. I murdered a mother and her son' Monkwood said no longer smiling, the haunted expression returning, etched in his face.

'And yet you allude to having more than that to tell me, Mr. Monkwood' Billy replied 'so digress because time is one thing you no longer have'

'Time is all I got' Monkwood replied, biting his finger again. 'Is it bugged in here, do they film what goes on?' Billy had never really thought about it, never even been asked the question, but he knew the answer all the same.

'No, no they can't do that Mr. Monkwood and even if they did, it would be inadmissible in court anyway, why?' Billy asked him.

'I'm not interested in whether it's admissible in court or not Mr. Preston' Monkwood replied, now showing a semblance of animation 'I just need to know that what I am about to tell you won't leave these four walls, Mr. Preston, that's all'

'I can assure you, Mr. Monkwood, whatever you tell me stays in here and in here' he said, pointing towards his temple. 'You're not recording?' Monkwood asked him

'I will need to record what we discuss yes, but if there is something you want to talk about off the record, then that's OK with me' Billy answered. He was desperate to find out where this was leading and to gain Monkwood's trust. This man had a story or at least thought he did and whatever it was, Billy wanted to hear it. It was his job to understand.

'I had to kill that poor woman and her son' he said, beginning to cry 'I had no choice, he made me do it'

The statement matched with Monkwood's sudden outburst of tears confused and disorientated Billy.

'Who, who made you do it, who made you do what?' Billy asked.

'My wife and my Daughter, they've gone, they're missing' Monkwood answered, composing himself. 'I had the call, the man called me and told me he had them, I had to find two people, kidnap them and play the game out, like I did, it was all staged' Billy was taken aback, this was until a moment a go an open and shut case. The man in front of him had kidnapped and murdered, of that there could be no denial and indeed, was no denial from Mr. Monkwood, but what he was being told changed things, moved the goal posts to the other end of the field.

'You mean you had to do those things to get your own family back, but why?' Billy responded.

'I DON'T KNOW' Monkwood screamed at him 'I don't know, he just said I would get them both back if I carried it out, I did as I was told, I want to see my family again' Monkwood said putting his head in his hands.

'I don't understand why you haven't told the police this' Billy asked 'they can help you'

'No, NO' Monkwood shouted 'The man made it very clear, if I say anything then my family die, I'll get them back in 72 hours, less than that now. I can wait it out.'

'You're taking the word of a maniac who made you kill two people, you're leaving the lives of you wife and child in his hands, can you afford to take that risk?' Billy pleaded with Monkwood to see some sense.

'Can I afford NOT to take that risk?' Monkwood responded, staring right into Billy's face.

'I think you need to make the police aware, they can act covertly and look for your family for you without what you've just said being public knowledge' Billy begged again 'Jesus they may even be able to catch this man' he said with exasperation in his tone.

'It's not your family, Mr. Preston, and you don't look old enough to even understand' Monkwood said 'let me ride it out a couple of days, I can do that, and when they're back, I'll tell everybody and so will my wife' he stared at the floor again 'I don't want to talk any longer Mr. Preston, there is nothing more to say, I did it and will never live with it, I've ruined my life and the lives of others to save my family and you would do the same' Monkwood paused 'you can go now' he finished

Billy Preston left his seat without saying a word and vacated the small white cell a different man to the one who had entered. He knew whoever had put Mr. Monkwood up to this, if indeed there had been someone, they would never let his wife and daughter leave whilst they had a scapegoat and that was what Monkwood was, holed up in this cell.

Just a few hours later Billy Preston was introducing himself to Chief Anthony Leith in sunny Edgartown.

'I need to talk to you about my Client, Barry Monkwood' Billy explained.

The chief rocked back in his seat, his hands behind his head.

'It never ceases to amaze me you know' he responded, leaning forward in his chair and placing the palms of his hands on the desk in front of him 'how you guys will literally represent any damn person'

'I'm acting for the State, Chief' Billy replied 'I don't get a choice of who I defend, I just do my job to the best of my ability'

'I bet you do' the chief sneered 'even if it means defending someone who's murdered a man's family and ripped a hole in this town.'

It was that last sentence which resonated more with Billy. It was almost as if the damage Monkwood had done to the town meant more to the chief than the what had been done to the victims.

Billy was wrong though. What sat with the Chief more than anything else, sat in his stomach like a boulder, was the fact they'd been to Monkwood's house. Knowing they'd interviewed the right man in the first place, the same man who the following day had spoken to the Chief in town, it stuck in his craw and was in danger of eating away at him. The Chief felt as though he had let the town down, he was their protector. The one time he'd been given the opportunity to do something more than deal with a traffic offence and he felt as though he'd blown it. However disappointed the townsfolk were in him would never match the way he felt about himself.

'What if I were to tell you my client had a motive Chief' Billy said, leaning forward in the chair himself.

'Would have to be some motive, to do that to a man's family, some motive' the chief responded, unwavering at the Lawyer's sudden candor. Billy continued.

'My Client has a wife and child too Chief, where are they?' Billy asked, laying the bait for the Chief.

'Not where he told us they were that's for sure, they're currently listed as missing' the Chief replied, oblivious of where the conversation was leading him 'We have a team excavating the rear garden as we speak, there was a patch of new soil there, looks ominous to be honest'

Now it was Billy who was caught off guard. He couldn't imagine Barry Monkwood had time to do a spot of gardening recently and the advent of new soil in the garden did strike him as more than a little odd. He thought for a moment and continued on the trajectory he had been going. Whilst he had the confidentiality of his client on his mind he knew he had to let the Chief know what he had been told, it could be more than relevant.

For the next five minutes the Chief sat there experiencing a mixed bag of emotions as Billy Preston divulged Barry Monkwoods story. The Chief couldn't quite believe the tale, it sounded too surreal, too farfetched to be true. On the other hand it added a semblance of understanding to why a seemingly reasonable member of the community had flipped and murdered two of the townsfolk for no obvious reason. People didn't just do that sort of thing for nothing other than kicks, did they?

Once Billy had finished relaying the information, the Chief tipped back in his chair again, thinking deeply, his hands clasped together to a point, his fingertips resting on his chin.

'OK, say it's true, say Monkwood did this as part of some kind of challenge, a way to get his own family back, where's the guarantee he would get them back and why not risk contacting us, the police? It makes no sense' The Chief responded, still trying to digest what had been told to him.

'You said that when you visited him he told you his wife and child were staying in the city with her mother?' Billy answered.

'Yes, but that's not telling us anything is it, that's not suggesting she's been abducted' the Chief replied.

'No, of course, it's not, but perhaps he thought you would investigate that line of enquiry, perhaps he thought you'd look into the story enough to see it wasn't true' Billy said.

This got the Chiefs back up and he felt instantly riled. A lot had been said about the force and indeed him personally in the past two days and he had no intention of taking the blame for this as well.

'Hang on one damn minute' the chief snapped back 'you know as well as I do if this story is true then he wouldn't have wanted us finding anything out, because it would have blown the cover and put his family's life at risk'.

'Exactly' Billy said smiling. 'I think he may have been telling the truth'

'That's not getting him out of Prison though, Mr. Preston' the Chief answered. He thought for a moment and then raised a question that had been on his mind since the discovery of the bodies 'Why did he have to murder them so brutally, if he's not a murderer I mean, but someone forced to do it?' the Chief asked 'why do it so outrageously'

Billy pondered the question briefly. 'I guess I'll get round to asking him that question, but my thoughts are, that's how he was told to do it. He stuck to what he was being asked to do, to the letter, in an attempt to get his family back, that's all I can assume' Billy said.

'Never assume' the Chief answered, just as the telephone on the desk broke the air with its chimes.

'Chief Anthony Leith' he answered, before listening briefly. He looked at Billy as he spoke 'I'll be right over' he put the phone back on the cradle, his complexion turning a pale grey.

'You'll need to see this, they've uncovered two bodies in Monkwood's garden, looks like you can forget your theory, we have a real fucking nutball on our hands' the Chief said.

Chapter Ten

Detectives Ashworth and Rosemount burst into Monkwood's cell in tandem, causing him to flinch at the sudden interruption to the silence.

Ashworth launched himself across the room and grabbed Monkwood round the throat.

'OK Scumbag time to talk' he shouted loudly in their prisoners face. Monkwood couldn't comprehend what was happening; as far as he was concerned they knew they had their man, what more was there for him to explain? Rosemount said nothing as Ashworth dragged Monkwood to the ground and led him through to the interview room.

His young inexperienced Lawyer, Billy Preston and the Chief of Edgartown's Police Department Anthony Leith stood in the corner of the room.

Detective Rosemount switched the digital recorder on.

'Time is twelve forty five pm, in presence are the detainee Mr. Barry Monkwood, Mr. Monkwood's Lawyer Mr. Billy Preston, the Chief of Edgartown Police Department Mr. Anthony Leith and Detectives Ashworth and Rosemount of the Massachusetts Police Department' Rosemount finished speaking and Ashworth lent over the chair opposite from where Monkwood was seated with his Lawyer.

'Now tell us the full story' Ashworth said. Monkwood looked confused.

'I don't understand' he said 'you know what happened'

'We know what you told us, Mr. Monkwood' Ashworth said 'however we don't know what happened, we do know what you told your Lawyer though' Monkwood glared angrily at Billy.

'You were meant to respect my confidentiality'

The Chief could take it no more, he wanted to put his hands around Monkwood's throat and throttle him until he turned blue, he could practically feel himself doing it. His knuckles shone white from clenching his fists so tightly and he finally exploded.

'You're rights went out the fucking window the moment we dug up the bodies of your wife and daughter from your garden this morning you sick fuck!' spittle flying from his mouth as he uttered the last syllable.

The words echoed around Monkwood's head as well as the interview room like a steam train bashing around inside his skull. It could not be, the voice on the phone had told him, the voice had assured him.

'They've been dead for days' Ashworth said coldly. Monkwood felt dizzy, his stomach knotted with nausea. He tried to speak but nothing evolved from his mouth. Suddenly he let out a guttural scream and began repeatedly smashing his head on the desk in front of him, his forehead instantly splitting and splashing the wood with flecks of blood. Billy Preston lurched out of the way as the Chief and Ashworth restrained Monkwood from behind and dragged him back to his cell. Blood streaming from his wound they threw him on the floor, shutting and locking the door behind them. Monkwood lay curled up on the floor in the fetal position sobbing silently.

'Don't you think we should clean up his head?' the Chief asked.

'Fuck him he can wait' Ashworth said as he walked back to the interview room. Anthony remained, looking at Monkwood through the viewing hatch in the door.

The two detectives, the chief and the Lawyer reconvened in the interview room.

'I have to say, he didn't react like somebody who knew his wife and daughter were already dead' Billy Preston said.

'You guys are always looking for an angle, a way out' Ashworth said. 'Face it, he's as guilty as sin'

'He has a point though' Rosemount said 'That was like no reaction I've ever seen, he seemed genuinely shocked'

'He's a fucking loony tune you know what these crackpots are like, he probably doesn't even remember, has some kind of split personality, he's crazy, end of' Ashworth said, seemingly drawing the argument to a conclusion with his final word.

They were all unconvinced though, especially the chief, something didn't seem right about the whole thing. What if Monkwood had been telling the truth to his Lawyer?

'Well forensics will pick up any anomalies I am sure' the Chief said. Ashworth laughed at this.

'There won't be any this is an open and shut case. It's clear as day'

There was a knock on the door and then a pause as someone waited to be given permission to enter.

A young lady walked in and beckoned over Detective Rosemount, whispering something in her ear before leaving the room.

'OK Chief, Mr. Preston, we'll charge Mr. Monkwood later and go from there, thanks for coming in today Chief' Rosemount said, signaling an end to their current involvement. Ashworth shook the hands of both men and directed them out and then joined Rosemount back in the interview room.

'What's going on?' he asked, sensing her sudden change in demeanor.

'A body has been discovered in the Marriot Hotel, they think it may be that reporter Mickey Henderson.'

The following day the press were all over the story, not least of all The Massachusetts Times. In the space of just a few days five people had been murdered; four from the same town and now a reporter from the city press. The police had released no information other than Henderson's Body had been found, however, the press immediately tied this to the story he'd ran about the Edgartown abductions and concluded he had met his unfortunate demise through some interconnected foul play.

'They make me sick' Ashworth said, tossing the newspaper down on the desk. 'Immediately assume the two things are associated, but that's not necessarily the case is it? They don't report the news, they speculate on it' he finished.

'Well that may be so but you and I both know those murders are somehow tied to this, forensics will confirm I am sure' Rosemount responded. 'And anyway' she continued 'we've already been told by the check in there someone had been staying in that room for a while, paying in cash and it wasn't Henderson'

'Have we got the CCTV footage yet?' Ashworth asked her.

'No the hotel are going through it to try and find a shot of the guy who stayed in that room. The Police Artist is also attempting to get a description as well' Rosemount replied.

'Pointless' Ashworth huffed, 'It's going to be Monkwood anyway.'

'I don't think it is,' Rosemount responded, getting tired of Ashworth's relentless desire to start a fight. 'He's owned up to the first two deaths, or the first two we knew of, but not the others, why not if he did them?'

Ashworth rolled his eyes at her and shook his head in a condescending manner, as if he were about to chastise a child.

'Think about it, his whole motive, his alibi is based on the supposed fact he murdered Mrs. Bradfield & her Son on the pretense he was doing it to protect his own wife and child' Ashworth answered 'If he admits to murdering them and the hack then where does he go, at the moment the guy has a tenuous grip on plausibility'

Rosemount knew that for all his misdirected rage and misogynistic attitude Ashworth was more than likely correct.

'Yeah I guess you have a good point' she painfully admitted 'but in saying that don't you think Monkwood has been overwhelmingly distraught since we broke the news to him yesterday, the guy hasn't stopped crying' she said.

The two Detectives stood for a while without saying anything, Ashworth flicking through the newspaper to find the sports section. He suddenly stopped rifling through the paper and looked up at Rosemount.

'That's true' he said 'Yet I've not heard a solitary peep out of him all morning'

The two Detectives made their way down to Monkwoods cell.

'Rise and shine animal' Ashworth shouted as he threw open the door. Monkwoods limp body hung from the bed sheets, wrapped tightly around his neck, the other end secured to the taps on the sink. His face blue his eyes rolled back in his head and his tongue lolling out the side of his mouth, he'd clearly been dead for some time.

Monkwood had somehow managed to wrap the bed sheets around the taps on the sink to form a make shift noose and had literally hung himself from the basin. It looked awkward and it looked slow. This hadn't been an easy suicide.

'FUCK' Ashworth screamed, kicking the door as he did 'Fucking asshole, gets away with it, he gets away with it, nobody gets justice now, nobody' he finished storming out of the cell.

Rosemount contemplated the floor, unable to look as Monkwoods dead face any longer.

'Oh Jesus' she said shaking her head at the cold, tiled ground.

Chapter Eleven

'What's for dinner?' John Sanders said as he entered the house.

'Hi Mum, how are you?' Gloria said smiling at him. John bounded over and kissed her on the cheek, hugging her at the same time

'Sorry, hi Mum, what's for dinner?' John was a cheeky, confident young man who had benefited from one of life's rare luxuries, a stable family home life.

His dad Mike worked as an extremely wealthy investment banker in the city and despite the economic downturn had always been a variable success. Gloria, John's Mother, had never had to work.

At twenty-one, despite having qualifications and the brain to do something with them, John had still failed to find a foothold in life. There was no obvious notion regarding what he would do as a career. Much to Mike's disappointment John had never shown any inclination to join him in banking, despite the offer being there. Mike was now a senior partner and could call the shots at a whim, but that didn't matter to John, he had no intention of going down the same road as his dad.

Mike wouldn't have minded too much if his son had shown some kind of ambition elsewhere, but there was nothing. Despite his academic qualities Mike hated to admit it, but John was becoming a disappointment to him. Not it would seem to Gloria though, John was and always would be the shining light in her eye. As far as she was concerned he could do no wrong.

'Dinner will be about an hour, your dad is going to be late' Gloria said.

'I'm starving now' John said, practically whining.

'Well I'm sure you'll live' Gloria said laughing 'why don't you take Pipet for a walk?' Pipet was the family Dog, a Labrador they'd had for fifteen years now. He was an old boy but liked nothing more than a trot along the Edgartown beeches. They'd brought Pipet for John when he was just a child and watched the two of them grow together. John had more of a bond with that dog than anybody else.

'Yeah OK saves me doing it later I guess' John said resignedly.

'You be careful out there,' Gloria called as the two bounded after each other out the front door. John laughed at that, calling back to her 'Nothing ever happens out here Mum' running off down the driveway with Pipet happily galloping in tow.

Until recently Gloria had thought the same. First the terrible murders of the two Bradfield family members and then the revelation that Barry Monkwood was responsible and had killed his own family as well. The whole town were in shock, everybody knew Barry Monkwood, he'd clowned around at many a kids party. Everybody knew the Bradfields as well. It was just awful and none of them could comprehend why this would happen in their peaceful town. There were plenty of rumors flying around but with all but Mr. Bradfield dead and Monkwood unlikely to reveal his motives she figured the truth would probably never out. Edgartown didn't have a crime rate, it didn't have crime and to be faced with four murders in the space of days was beyond imaginable. Horrifying to the extreme her husband had said and he was right.

Picking up a large wooden spoon, Gloria stirred the casserole in the slow cooker as the front door slammed behind her, causing her to jump. The thoughts of Monkwood and his evil crimes had spooked her.

'Hi Honey' Mike said, putting his suit jacket on the coat rack before stealing in for a kiss. At 47 years of age he was still a good looking man, rugged, George Clooney-esque Gloria felt. At least that was what she thought. Mike on the other hand felt as though he was fifty-seven and looked sixty seven despite Gloria regularly telling him that beauty was in the eye of the beholder.

'Just heard on the radio, Monkwood killed himself this morning, found him in his cell' Mike said, routing around in the fridge for something to snack on before dinner.

'God that's awful' Gloria said, continuing to stir the casserole in an hypnotic trance.

'Not really, brings an end to the sorry matter' Mike said in a matter of fact way. 'Did you see the paper today as well, they found that reporter yesterday too, they think Monkwood was responsible for that as well, that Henderson guy.'

'None of it makes sense to me,' Gloria replied 'why would somebody do that, flip and so randomly as well?'

'Why do people do what they do?' Mike said 'we'll never understand the human mind we're not meant to' He'd finally found something unhealthy to munch on, a chocolate biscuit 'we're all such unpredictable animals'

'Hey, you leave room for dinner, I've been slaving over this all day' Gloria said.

'It's only a biscuit' Mike replied 'and anyway, nobody slaves over a slow cooker, that's why I bought it for you' He laughed at himself and made his way from the kitchen through to the front room. 'Oh and they're speculating in the press that Monkwood wouldn't have stopped, wanted to be some kind of notorious serial killer'

'Thank God he's gone then' Gloria said, re-covering the pot 'it makes my skin crawl to think of the number of children' parties he attended, the amount of homes he was allowed in to'

The door knocking momentarily distracted her. 'That was quick' she said to nobody 'he's always forgetting his keys' As Gloria opened the door she saw enough to visualize a man putting something over her face before she passed out instantly. Dropping her body to the floor the masked man made his way into the house. Mike was watching television with his back to the door, the news reporting on events in Edgartown over the past few days.

'Unbelievable isn't it?' he said, looking up as the man towering above him covered his face with the same rag. Mike took a longer to pass out, fighting hard against the towering strength above him. Eventually the man stood in the front room looking over Mikes unconscious body, slumped in the chair. Gloria lay in the hallway and the man stood, silently staring as the news continued to relay recent events in the background.

'Hey Tommy,' John said at the tall lanky guy trotting along the beach. 'What you doing?'

'What the fuck does it look like I'm doing?' Tommy replied breathlessly, stopping as he hunched over and put his hands on his thighs. 'Jogging.'

'You've never come across an exercise freak before,' John said.

Tommy looked over at the dog, running up the beach.

'Yeah we'll you never struck me as a dog walker, each to their own aye.'

'You were going some' John said, still trying to maintain the mindless small talk.

'How'd you mean?' Tommy asked, still trying to catch his breath.

'That was flat out running, not jogging' John continued.

'So fucking what' Tommy replied 'What are you, my nutritionist?' At that, Tommy raced away again into the dusk.

'Miserable prick' John said, making his way back along the beach. He called Pipet and the two of them climbed the steep embankment and onto the street. Before too long John's house was in sight and his stomach rumbled an appreciative growl, reminding him that he was still hungry. His dads BMW was resting in the driveway and John was immediately pleased, not that his dad was home, but that dinner would be imminent.

Routing around for his keys, which for once he'd remembered to take with him, John made his way into the house.

'What's for dinner?' he said laughing, recalling the conversation with his mum earlier. Nobody answered.

The television played to itself in the living room but nobody was in there and the kitchen wafted the distinct aroma of a chicken casserole, yet nobody appeared to be home.

'Oh shit' John said under his breath. He had a sudden fear that his mum and dad were upstairs making the most of quiet time without John being around and he contemplated leaving for a while and coming back. Realizing the house was deafly silent, with the exception of his own breathing, John decided otherwise.

'Mum, dad?' he called into the darkness at the top of the stairs. There were no lights on at all up there it seemed. Placing his foot on the first step he contemplated and then said to himself 'Idiot'

He realized his parents were most likely in the garden having a crafty glass of wine before dinner. They often sat out on the veranda, especially if it was a nice evening, which it was. Venturing through the front room and the patio doors in the dining room, John made his way out into the garden. The sound of the nearby waves crashed but nobody was there in the garden either.

For whatever reason John was acutely aware that something wasn't sitting right with him. He couldn't put his finger on it but felt scared. He had no idea why. At twenty-one years of age he was in no place to be scared but despite all seeming well, something bothered him.

Looking around the garden John figured out what it was. Over the past few days he'd heard nothing but horror stories of murder in his little town and even though they'd got the guy, it must have unsettled him more than he realized. How often do people you know go crazy and then kill other people you actually know? He imagined not very often at all in the grand scheme of things.

Deciding to check the rooms above, John made his way back into the house and began to venture up the dark stairs. He was acutely aware of the overbearing silence again as he climbed those dark steps. John wasn't afraid of the dark, not much more than anyone else, but the fact the light switch was situated upstairs had always bothered him. He'd never been anywhere before where the upstairs lights couldn't be switched on until you got to the top of the stairs. The more he thought about it the more dangerous he realized it was. No wonder he had fallen down them so many times as a kid.

Climbing the stairs much slower than was necessary John finally reached the half way point. He was self aware enough to realize he was practically creeping up them and he was also aware he was now engulfed with darkness as the residue light from downstairs dimmed below him. Suddenly John's heart stopped. At the top of the stairs a pair of eyes stared at him, caught glinting in the light drifting from the hallway below. John looked straight into them. It was as though someone was crouched at the top of the stairs waiting to pounce. John didn't know whether to run back down, go up them or scream. He realized he was now incredibly frightened. Someone was watching him.

Continuing to climb the steps John could hear his heartbeat thudding through his inner ear, increasing his fear with every pump. Suddenly Pipet bolted out of the shadows down the stairs and past John, who almost fell down them as he did.

'Jesus Pipet I almost shit my pants' John said, realizing it was the damn dogs eyes he'd been looking at all along. The fear that raged through him just a moment ago was instantly gone, and John stood on the steps feeling foolish and silly.

Racing the remaining steps John switched the light on. That palpable fear instantly returned, engulfing his every sense. If he'd thought he was scared as he looked into those phantom eyes, that was nothing compared to what he saw. Scrawled on the wall in thick black marker pen were the words 'I had to take them'

Chapter Twelve

Detectives Rosemount and Ashworth sat at their desk as Brian Radzinski placed the small cassette in the player.

'And this was on Henderson when they found him?' Ashworth asked, leaning forward in his chair.

'Yep, it's his Dictaphone. Most reporters have them, although nowadays they use digital,' Radzinski said.

For the next ten minutes the three of them proceeded to listen to the material on the cassette. Once it had finished none of them spoke, they listened as the man who had clearly murdered Henderson left the room and heard the audible click of the hotel room door as he closed it behind him. The hissing of the cassette tape was all that could now be heard, not a single sound otherwise, apart from the faint distant tooting of car horns out on the street at the time.

'That was eerie,' Rosemount said, finally breaking the silence 'Hearing a man's death like that, it was worse than seeing it I think.'

Radzinski nodded, Ashworth said nothing.

'That clearly wasn't Monkwood,' Ashworth eventually spoke.

'No but whoever it was had a similar story to Monkwood, we need to check records,' Rosemount replied.

'We're assuming, of course, the guy who killed Henderson was telling the truth and hasn't been working with Monkwood' Radzinski chipped in.

This prompted Ashworth in his usual imitable fashion to thank Radzinski for his assistance and wave him away. Radzinski duly obliged, leaving Rosemount and Ashworth alone in the office.

'You can be quite rude sometimes,' Rosemount said

'I don't like him, he's Canadian,' Ashworth responded, as if that were reason enough alone to dislike Radzinski.

'Oh and racist as well then' Rosemount continued without a hint of humor. Ashworth didn't even attempt to deny this, he didn't want to.

'We have a real problem on our hands here,' Ashworth said 'We're looking for Henderson's killer now and we need to consider the possibility that Monkwood did not kill his wife and Daughter' Ashworth looked perplexed.

'If there really was somebody out there pulling the strings then they're still out there' Rosemount responded, looking equally as concerned as Ashworth now was.

'We have to find Henderson's killer first of all, it may lead us to the instigator of this madness' Ashworth answered.

'Well we can start by looking into similar cases from a couple of years ago in Florida' Rosemount said 'if the voice on the cassette was telling the truth then it shouldn't be too hard to find who they were'

'OK I'll contact Tom Welling over in the Florida PD, he's a friend of mine from way back and if anybody knows of a possible history here it will be him' Ashworth said 'Anyway may be an idea to bring him in, he's one of the best Criminologists out there'

'OK good thinking' Rosemount said. She was well aware of who Tom Welling was, she'd read about him the press many times, he was quite a figure in his neck of the woods, she had no idea Ashworth and Tom were acquaintances though. Despite Wellings reputation it concerned Rosemount slightly that Wellings friendship with Ashworth could result in the case being hindered. As it now appeared Monkwood was perhaps a smaller cog in a bigger wheel and none of them could afford to be complacent. Five people were dead already and only God knew where this would end if they didn't focus one hundred percent on the case in hand. While Rosemount thought of Welling and the possible problem of him being there, she had become oblivious to Ashworth being on the phone. He finished the call and turned around to face her.

'There's been another abduction, it's in Edgartown again' Ashworth said, dreaded seriousness etched on his brow 'what the fuck is going on over there?' he concluded. The two officers made their way out of the office ready to take the short trip over to Edgartown yet again.

Oakwood Police Departments finest, Eric Blane, made his way up the stairs of the Sanders home while Officer Clearwater and Chief Anthony Leith discussed the situation with the traumatized John Sanders.

'Sure we'll find your mum and dad soon' Anthony lied. He didn't want to tell John what he really thought, that this could well be swimming its way up shit creak with the Bradfield's Family. He didn't want to tell John he had no idea what to do and where to start given the fact Monkwood, the previous culprit, had garroted the last living air out of his lungs in a Massachusetts Police cell. He also didn't want to admit he was glad the Detectives from Boston were on their way over. For all the excitement Anthony had recently craved from his position he figured he'd had enough in the past few days, now all he really needed was to see things go back to the way they had been before. The intervention of the Boston Detectives was a welcome one, Anthony knew he was out of his league with this and now the whole situation had shifted once again he had even less of a clue what was going on than before.

John Sander sat there looking dazed, confused, overwhelmed and in total shock.

'You got the guy that did this before, the clown guy?' he finally said, looking at Anthony for answers.

'We did yes' Jenny answered for him.

'Whoever did this' Blane shouted from down the stairs 'is a retard that's for sure, looks like this writing here has been done by a two year old blind albino' he continued, laughing hysterically at his own comment. Nobody else mustered a smile.

'Why did you invite that buffoon here again?' Jenny asked Anthony. He glared sheepishly up at her.

'Because he's my friend Jenny and a man of the law, he has his own ways but they work believe me'

'Well so far all I've seen him do is use the toilet an uncomfortable amount of times, eat enough to solve Third World famine and make rash references' Jenny replied, agitated that Anthony didn't appear to see Blanes faults the same way she did 'and, what the hell does Albino have to do with it anyway?' she concluded, looking angry. Anthony smiled and shook his head. He didn't know either.

John Sanders was oblivious to the conversation the officers were having, he continued to stare at nothing in particular.

'You got the guy?' he said again, his voice rising slightly with a querying tone 'so who is doing this?' Nobody spoke because none of them had any idea what the answer was.

Detectives Ashworth and Rosemount arrived not long afterwards. Ashworth gave the house the once over and found nothing of any consequence other than the literal writing on the wall. He asked Anthony to step outside and the two officers of different ranks and backgrounds made their way out into the sunshine lit front garden.

'I'll tell you something about this place, it's always so damn sunny' Ashworth said, as if that was a negative point.

'Not a big fan of the sun then?' Anthony replied, intending to continue the small talk. Apparently Ashworth had raised a rhetorical point and had no intention of continuing further.

'There was a tape on Henderson, the reporter, I won't bore you with the detail but Monkwood didn't kill him, we're looking for someone else' Ashworth said.

'Bore me with the detail' Anthony responded, 'I'm the chief of police over here after all' it was a digging remark and he'd meant it to be. Ashworth nodded his head in the direction of the sea, indirectly towards the city.

'Yeah but not over there you're not' he replied without intended vitriol but the words stung all the same. 'You really don't need to know too much other than Monkwood had, to an extent been telling the truth, the voice on the tape confirmed that, he was carrying out someone else's orders and there's nothing to say that whoever has taken the Sanders family isn't doing the same' Ashworth continued.

'So where does that leave us then other than with absolutely no leads' Anthony asked.

'It leaves Rosemount and I with a lot of work to do and we'd appreciate yours and your colleagues help. You know these people round here' Ashworth said.

Anthony took exception to being the help, it was his town after all but he guessed that Ashworth had a point. Anthony was bitterly aware of exactly what they had failed to achieve last time and the intervention of the city police was always going to be welcoming if not a slight kick in the teeth.

'We do have a lead anyway, the guy on the tape said the same thing happened to his family over in Florida' Ashworth continued 'I have a friend down there in the force, he's a top criminologist, his name is Tom Welling. Figured he may have some knowledge of what's going on here and if he don't, he can certainly gain some, the man's a genius' At that Ashworth turned around and made his way back into the house. Anthony figured the conversation was over then, not that there had been much conversing on his part. So it had been decided, Anthony and his team of seemingly inept local officers would be nothing more than a go between for the outsiders and the townsfolk. He made his way back inside the house just in time to hear Eric Blane announce 'There's something wrong with the flusher on your toilet, it won't go down'

Anthony couldn't help smile to himself as he shook his head, it seemed Ashworth had a valid point.

Chapter Thirteen

The glare of the sunshine filtered through the blinds and invaded Tom Welling's still closed eyes with glaring pin pointed accuracy. Not for the first time this week or undoubtedly the last, he was awaking to a thunderous hangover. Given the amount of alcohol he tended to consume on a daily basis he was forever shocked at his body's total inability to deal with constant intrusion of alcohol in his blood. By no means an alcoholic, Tom had become steadily dependent on alcohol with every meal and deep into every evening. Marie his wife, lay quietly still next to him. She wasn't unaware of his heavy drinking but it affected his overall behavior so minimally that it was always hard to tell if he was drunk or not. The unflinching litmus test was always the way he felt the following morning.

Tom opened his eyes fully letting the light take over his retinas. His head pounded from all angles, the ache practically impossible to pin point its actual location in his skull. It felt as though a thousand bees were swarming around his brain and his mouth was nothing more than desert sand.

'Why do I do this to myself?' he muttered as he swung his legs out the side of the bed, gingerly placing the soles of his feet on the warm carpet and rising like the undead. Much the same as a zombie in an old horror picture he staggered across the bedroom and out the door, barely making it down the stairs to the kitchen. His son sat at the breakfast table eating whatever cereal sat in the porcelain bowl.

'You look like shit dad'. A nice greeting to start the day off and pretty choice words for a sixteen year old kid as well but Tom figured Sean was right.

'Morning Sean I feel it, you off to school now?' Sean left his bowl where it was, mum could get that later, threw on his worn and torn rucksack and an equally worn cap. 'Yep' he said in response.

'Those three empty bottles of wine sitting in the trash yours?' he smiled. Tom smiled back in return.

'Piss off you little piss taker and have a good day at school' he laughed as Sean made his way out of the kitchen and down the hall.

It said a lot that Tom was in the habit of being routinely lectured by his sixteen year old Son, but it was becoming an unfortunate and somewhat embarrassing habit. The slamming of the front door, always done with far more force than was necessary and probably a deliberate affront to his hangover was simultaneously met by the ringing of the telephone. Literally everything seemed so much louder when the head was marinated in alcohol induced dehydration.

Removing the telephone from the cradle Welling gingerly pressed it to his ear.

'Hello,' he said, hoping that whoever was on the other end was at best a wrong number and would hang up.

'Hello Tom,' Ashworth said. 'Been a long while' and indeed it had, some years in fact but despite his muffled head Welling was immediately aware of who he was speaking to, he'd known Ashworth a long time.

'Blow me, Graham Ashworth, who died?' Welling asked him, his hangover seeming to disperse immediately. The sudden adrenalin rush of speaking to an old yet genuine friend, helped to dissipate the awful feeling that had engulfed him since he awoke.

'Five people so far,' Ashworth laughed down the phone at Welling's memory.

It had been an ongoing joke between the two of them for many years, back when Welling resided in good old Boston. If he heard his friend's voice on the other end of the phone then he was reasonably sure Ashworth was going to need him to find some butchering psycho, and invariably that was the case. So for a long time he had taken to beginning all of his calls with the ironically immortal words of 'Who Died?' and on this occasion that couldn't have been more appropriate.

'How you been anyway?' Ashworth continued. 'Been a long long time.'

'Too long actually, on both our parts, time just seems to fly doesn't it as you get older?' Welling said 'I'll tell you something though, whatever you've got in those dulcet tones of yours should be marketed by a pharmaceutical because my hangover has sure as shit wandered right off the face of my…well face' he said.

Ashworth laughed, 'It really is good to hear your voice Tom, the family doing well?'

'Well they're still here Graham so I must be doing something right'

'Listen we'll catch up properly later Tom but I really need to know if you're available to get over to Boston and look at a case for me, we think it's, no we know it's linked to something that happened in Florida a few years back' Ashworth said.

Tom looked at the calendar on the kitchen wall, out of habit more than anything else, he knew there was nothing on it. It was the same as someone not wearing a watch and looking at their wrist for the time. Tom knew he had no work he hadn't been contacted since he'd failed to solve a big murder case. Turning up each day with a hangover had no doubt played a part. If it weren't for Marie's work they'd be destitute now which made him pissing away what money they did have even more deplorable.

'Listen Graham I have to be honest with you, I haven't worked for nearly a year, I may not be the best man for you right now' Welling spoke honestly. As much as he needed the work he didn't need to let his friend down in the process.

'So you're available?' was all Ashworth answered with 'great, well listen we've got a guy here who is, well it's complicated, but we had a guy who kidnapped a couple of people, gave the husband three days to choose which one to kill, oh I tell you what I'll explain it when you get here, it's all a little fucked up'

Welling felt cold, the blood in his veins coursed through him like ice, he'd heard all of this before and he'd worked on the case.

'Jesus Graham same thing did happen here, not far from me, I worked on the damn case' Welling said.

'Yeah we know about the Peterson case, guy's family go missing, has to choose which one to save yada yada,' Ashworth said. 'What happened to that guy, Phil Peterson, his family never did come back?'

'That's right, we held him as a suspect for a while, I had a real strong gut feeling about that guy but nothing really stuck and the pieces didn't fit. He walked in the end,' Welling responded. 'Never did locate his family though, we couldn't have done any more really, they just vanished off the face of the earth and him, Peterson, haven't really thought about him for some time. He's become a distant memory,' Welling lied.

'Well not anymore Tom he's back on the scene, at least we think he is. Reporter here was murdered, had a tape recording the whole thing. The guy who killed him may be your guy Peterson. He still thinks his daughter at least is alive and waiting to come home.' Ashworth paused for a second 'We'll play you the tape when you get here but this thing is bigger than it ever was back there. Do you think you'll recognize his voice if you hear it?'

'Definitely, yes, I can't forget it,' Welling said. 'Sounds as though you have a real problem down there, you said five dead, or was that a joke?'

'Afraid not and it could be about to increase, we've had another abduction,' Ashworth answered 'Time really is of the essence, can you fly out today?'

'I'll have a look online but Graham, I can't afford the flights, times are hard, I can't afford anything right now' Welling said, not looking for sympathy, he didn't deserve it.

'No worries' Ashworth responded and then proceeded to give Welling his credit card details over the phone, 'Use them to book everything you need and I'll see you when you get here, we'll sort out a salary and expenses when you arrive'

They bid their farewells and Welling made his way up the stairs to Marie, his hangover now a forgotten memory.

'Who was that on the phone?' she asked as he made his way into the bedroom.

Welling spent the next ten minutes relaying the story to Marie and the following two hours packing his bag and booking a flight. By midday he was on the freeway making his way towards the Falmouth Airpark to catch a flight to Boston and reopen a can of worms he'd thought long since closed.

Chapter Fourteen

Phil Peterson climbed out of the shower and began to towel himself dry.

A meticulously clean and tidy man Phil took pride in his appearance and was always immaculately well groomed. Many people had commented that they believed him to be homosexual his vanity was so transparent. That couldn't have been further from the truth Phil had been or indeed was, to all intents and purposes, a married man. The only exception for Phil was that his wife of fifteen years had been missing for the past two of those, not to mention his Daughter as well.

For a man who had recently murdered someone in chillingly cold blood, Phil was rather chipper this morning.

The death of the reporter Mickey Henderson had given Phil a terrible choice to make but, as the voice on the phone had revealed to him, if he carried out the deed he would have his daughter returned to him.

Why should Phil believe the voice was anybody's guess, Phil had been lied to before. All hope, however, was in that voice and he'd spoken to his daughter this time as well. Phil knew in his heart that Barbara, his wife, was long gone and he'd grown to understand and accept that both she and his Daughter would be seen no more. Just as Phil had begun to come to terms with his loss the voice returned and the voice demanded once again. What did he want? Phil honestly didn't know. He'd asked many times why the voice targeted him, why that man wanted to make him do things, take his family away from him but the voice on the phone never gave him any answers, never made it clear. The voice just demanded over and over again, that he do the mans will and all would eventually be alright.

Phil buttoned up his crisp white shirt tucked it into his black trousers, fastened his slim black tie and slicked back his hair. He figured he looked pretty good for a man flirting with insanity. Recent events were beginning to take their toll on him but the voice had called again the evening before and one more challenge lay ahead. Then, finally, he would see the return of his daughter and finally the nightmare may be over.

Grabbing his dark black suit jacket from the back of the hotel room door, Phil threw it on and made his way out. He looked back at the room behind him, gazing at the very few personal belongings he had there and wondered if he would ever see any of those things again. He strongly doubted it.

The hotel corridor smelt aromatically of bacon, sausage and egg. That welcoming warm fragrance a cooked hotel breakfast gave. Phil was pretty sure they piped that smell into each room through the air vents, just to entice people downstairs to spend a little more on a plate of saturates to start the day.

Catching the elevator and making his way down to the foyer Phil Peterson climbed out on the lower level and attempted to make his way outside. His legs, however, had a different plan, the same plan his nose and stomach had joined in on.

'What the hell' he said only to himself and made the short trip across the foyer to the dining room, off the side of the lobby. As Phil snuck through the doorway the revolving glass door that was the entrance to East Falmouth's Admiralty Inn made it's symmetrically circular journey to welcome in a new patron. As Phil Peterson drifted out of sight, Tom Welling, green duffle bag on shoulder, appeared in the foyer. Neither man caught a glimpse of each other as each of them would have recognized the other for sure. Welling had worked closely with Peterson in the disappearance of his family. Welling was considered one of the finest Criminologists Florida had to offer but even he was unable to fathom out what had happened to Peterson's family. Phil Peterson had liked Welling. He showed endeavor, he wasn't willing to give up but eventually as the calls ceased and the disappearance became logged as one of those unsolved mysteries, Welling and Peterson had gone their separate ways.

Dumping his duffle bag down at reception Welling leaned over the counter and smiled a warm flirtatious grin at the young girl seated at the desk.

'Welcome to the Admiralty Inn' Janice, the name badge revealed, said, 'how can I help you today Sir?' Welling proceeded to give Janice his details, all the while chatting away about nothing in general with his usual charm, his confidence spurred on by the few drinks he'd consumed on the short hospitable flight to Boston.

Welling took his room key and made his way out of the foyer and into the elevator not long ago shared by Phil Peterson. It was an ironically and oddly small world after all perhaps.

Peterson meanwhile was tucking his way into a hearty and wholly unhealthy cooked breakfast. He figured as he masticated an encased piece of pig or sausage, as it's known, to a greasy pulp manageable for his esophagus, that there was a chance he may not be eating again any time soon, so he should get his fill now.

Finally finishing up with a swig of warm yet distinctly poor quality coffee, Peterson made his way over to the waitress and paid at the counter. After exchanging a few of the usual day-to-day pleasantries he embarked on the short walk outside and hailed a cab.

It appeared as though practically taxis alone habituated the entire street. Indeed it would have been harder to hail a standard pedestrian driven vehicle.

Peterson climbed into one of the few taxis which simultaneously pulled over to the sidewalk just as Tom Welling exited the building and entered the taxi directly behind.

'City Police Department please' Welling said.

'No problem' the taxi driver replied in a thick Boston drawl, 'you're not from round here?' the cab driver asked.

Welling was anti small talk, unless it was with a pretty hotel receptionist, of course, but he despised the needless chatter you invariably seem to get with every single taxi driver he encountered. Welling was well aware he appeared to turn into a gibbering mindless idiot every time his ass touched the seat of a cab. He already knew he would have to resist the temptation of the archetypal rhetoric's such as 'Have you been on long?', 'has it been busy?' and his favorite 'so, what time do you finish?' None of the questions held any substance and God knew Welling had absolutely no desire to care about the answers. He was always amazed at how those generic mundane questions to a cab driver could derive a passionate and voracious response, as if thirty passengers hadn't already asked them the same thing beforehand.

'Actually, I am from around here' Welling replied 'The Florida in me has kicked the Boston right out'

'Hey, you ain't kidding' The cab driver responded. 'So, you back home coz of good news or bad, because they're the only two reasons anyone ever ends up back home' he continued.

'Bad I guess' Welling answered. The Cab driver shook his head knowingly as if he'd half expected the answer.

'Yeah you know most people who end up home, it's usually because of bad news' he said, shaking his head. 'So if you don't mind me asking, what brings you back?'

'I'm a criminologist, it's work' Welling answered, looking out of the grimy cab window at the hustle and bustle of Boston life he was passing by.

'Right I see' the cab driver replied 'So you're one of those guys who can see into the minds of others, get what makes them tick?'

'That's pretty much it yes, in a roundabout way' Welling responded 'I'm working on a case out here'

'That Noah guy?' The cab driver asked him, looking at Welling in his rear-view mirror.

'Noah guy? I haven't heard about him no' Welling said.

'You know, this guy who's been abducting people two at a time, they're calling him Noah' cab driver said, chuckling slightly at the irony of it.

Welling was now more interested. 'Who exactly are 'they' who are calling him Noah?' he asked.

'The press, of course, came out with it this morning, due to the fact he kidnaps them two by two you know' he answered, looking at Welling again in his mirror.

'I see, that's clever I guess, in a sick way, but it's clever all the same' Welling said.

'Yeah well not half as clever as getting someone to do his dirty work for him, they thought they had the guy, they never did though' the cab driver shook his head as if in disbelief at what he'd just said 'fucking crazy son of a bitch' he concluded, still shaking his head in the same dumfounded fashion, so much so, Welling wondered how he could see where he was going.

'Well I guess in time we'll find out what's going on' Welling responded 'They'll catch this guy, they always slip up eventually'

'So you are working on this case then?' the cab driver asked inquisitively.

'That I can't say,' Welling replied, looking out of his window again as the city police department rolled into view.

'We're here' the cab driver said pulling the car to an unnecessary screeching halt.

Welling paid the fair, grabbed his bag from the trunk of the car and made his way into the police station. As he entered the door, a well-dressed, smart man with his back to him stood in the entrance as well, his arms outstretched as if he were about to embark on an operatic crescendo.

'I KILLED MICKEY HENDERSON,' he shouted at the top of his voice. 'I KILLED THE REPORTER,' he said now, even louder. The police officers in the large entrance hall seemed slow to react, possibly thinking this was yet another crack pot, of which there were always plenty when a murderer was on the loose. This was especially true when the murderer or in this case kidnapper was beginning to gain press notoriety.

Welling made his way up behind the man and cautiously rounded his side to face him. The man, his arms still outstretched looked Welling in the eye as Welling gazed back. Both men seemed as genuinely surprised as each other.

'You need to arrest me, Mr. Welling,' Phil Peterson said, beginning to smile, 'it's part of the rules.'

'Jesus Christ Phil, what have you done?' Welling asked.

'What I was told, Mr. Welling, what he told me to do'

Detectives Graham Ashworth and Cherry Rosemount appeared from behind and immediately cuffed Peterson and led him away. Ashworth looked back over his shoulder as they walked.

'Welcome back Tom, you may as well follow us down to the interview room, nothing like a baptism of fire aye?' he said, putting his thumb up to Welling. Welling nodded, attempting to recover from the shock of seeing a ghost from his past in close proximity, Welling tried to comprehend the words Peterson had spoken.

Phil Peterson sat quietly in the interview room looking decidedly relaxed for a man who had just admitted to a murder.

Welling stood behind the two way mirror watching Ashworth and Rosemount interview him. It had been a long time since he'd seen his buddy and he looked great, the Boston PD had clearly served him well. Welling focused his attention on the job in hand. Sitting there, looking as well dressed as ever and nonchalantly relaxed was Phil Peterson, someone else he hadn't set eyes on for some time.

'So Mr. Peterson' Ashworth said, staring at him as he traced the end of the pen he was holding across his lips 'you killed Mr. Henderson, the reporter did you?'

Peterson had waived his right to counsel, insisting he was happy to tell the whole truth and take which ever fall came his way.

'That is correct, I murdered him in the Marriot Hotel,' Peterson said.

Welling couldn't quite believe what he was hearing, Peterson sounded as though he was reading from a well-rehearsed script. As he watched Peterson's expressions, however, he saw nothing in them which suggested he was lying.

'Anyone who can read a newspaper or switch on a television will tell you Mr. Henderson was found in the Marriot Hotel Mr. Peterson,' Rosemount said. 'That does not necessarily mean they killed him. Make us believe you.'

Peterson smiled his relaxed grin, as if he were attending an interview for a vacancy rather than a murder enquiry. The confident grins were proving too much for Ashworth and he smashed the palms of his hands on the table, 'ENOUGH!' he screamed, causing Rosemount to jump. Not a hair on Peterson's well-groomed head moved and his smile never waned.

'Please Detective Ashworth you can no more frighten me than he can,' Peterson said, shifting his position in the chair to a more comfortable one.

'And who is he exactly?' Rosemount said in a calm, low tone.

'He is the one who took my family, my wife and daughter, two years ago,' Peterson said. 'And he is back,' he finished.

'I've looked at your file, Mr. Peterson,' Ashworth said. 'I know all about you and your story. It would seem you were the only suspect in the case, no motive, nobody else ever involved, in fact the only person who was ever considered the likely option, was you' Ashworth said, smiling himself now. This statement gained a reaction as the confident grin faded fast from Peterson's face.

'I can assure you Detectives' Peterson said in a calm and steady tone 'I did not abduct my wife and child.'

'I'm sure you did not,' Rosemount said, trying to pacify the situation.

'No, you just killed them both didn't you?' Ashworth said.

Welling continued to study Peterson, trying to gauge a reaction. Ashworth was right, Peterson had been the only suspect and Welling had always found him strange and slightly removed emotively from everything which was going on. There was never any evidence against Peterson apart from his cold disconnection to the fact his wife and daughter were missing. Welling had to admit though, that although his hunches had served him well in the past, with nothing to go on it was practically impossible to ever really charge Peterson with anything other than being a cold and seemingly callous person. That in itself was hardly a crime. Now that more abductions had been made and people were being murdered it made less sense for Peterson to be involved, however here he was, he had been brought back into the limelight. Welling considered that maybe that was the intention of whoever the perpetrator was, to give the police an individual to focus on now that Barry Monkwood had committed suicide and taken himself out of the loop.

'I'm not even dignifying that with a response, Mr. Welling will tell you, I had nothing to do with their disappearance' Peterson answered calmly. 'Now you wanted to know what had happened with Mr. Henderson I believe, the reason I am here?' Peterson said softly and with a marginal air of sarcasm.

'Indeed it is' Rosemount replied whilst Ashworth continued to stare unflinchingly at Peterson 'Please continue'

'OK, I received a call from the 'voice' the man who called years before and said he had my wife and daughter. I chose to save my daughter, did I ever tell you that?' Peterson said before continuing to speak, rather than await a response to his question. 'Anyway he told me he had kept his word and hadn't killed my little girl. He let me speak to her. You see the deal before was that I had to make a choice who would die, but he didn't ever tell me he would return the one who lived. He never did that.'

'And so you believe everything this man says to you?' Ashworth said.

'Yes, as would you if your family, your child, were relying on you to,' Peterson said, his tone very serious. 'He told me I had to do two things in order to get my daughter back, not just save her, get her back. The first was to come here and murder the reporter, which I duly did.'

'And the second, what was the second?' Rosemount asked, leaning forward in her seat.

'This,' Peterson said. 'Hand myself in to you and tell all. He wants you to know he's serious, he wants you to know he's real and he wants you to understand he will never stop. He has a taste for the game he's created. I was just the beginning, detectives. Now he wants to do this all the time. He'll never stop, until you stop him.' Peterson leaned forward in the chair as he said this, his face stony and deadly serious. He meant every word he said, he believed every syllable. Welling examined Peterson's every move and was convinced. Peterson was afraid of whoever was doing this without question.

'Detectives I just want my daughter back. I want this to end for me now, it's been going on long enough.' Peterson sat back in his chair, suddenly looking tired and weary.

'You're aware you're going to be spending a long time in jail for what you did to Mr. Henderson?' Rosemount said.

'Sacrificing my own freedom for that of my daughter?' Peterson responded. 'To me that's a no brainer Detective. I would do that any day of the week, of that you can be sure.'

'OK Peterson explain what happened to Mickey Henderson, tell us how you murdered him?' Ashworth asked. Welling continued to examine from behind the glass, this was what he'd really wanted to see. It was one thing to murder someone but something else to discuss how you did it. Welling had taken part in many conversations with psychotic serial killers and all of them took great pride and pleasure in describing their deeds. Most of them had wanted to be caught and mainly to gain the notoriety that came with it. Welling had also interviewed many people who had killed in self-defense or by accident and invariably, those people were full of remorse and didn't want to discuss things or relieve the act.

'You have Mr. Welling here?' Peterson asked suddenly, looking directly at the two way mirror in the interview room 'Of course you do' he said, responding to his own question. 'I have a great deal of admiration for Mr. Welling, nobody tried harder to locate my wife and child, even to the extent of believing I did it' Peterson continued to look at his own reflection in the two way mirror. 'Isn't that right, Mr. Welling?' he said to his own reflection.

Tom Welling nodded silently on the other side of the glass.

'I will tell everything to Mr. Welling if you wouldn't mind' Peterson said. 'No offence Detectives but I am sure you can peruse from the other side of the glass just as my old acquaintance is'

Ashworth and Rosemount left their chairs.

'Not a problem Peterson but you fuck around or try anything stupid, as you know, we're right through there' Ashworth said, gesturing towards the mirror.

'Why would I Detective? are you forgetting I came to you?' Peterson said, smiling again.

Ashworth and Rosemount left the interview room and made their way through the door to the viewing area. Welling was still watching Peterson through the glass.

'Well, what do you think?' Ashworth said as he entered the room.

'What do you think?' Welling answered with the same question.

'I think he is a cold, calculating, un-emotive fucker and I don't like him' Ashworth said.

'The very reasons I had him high on my list of suspects before' Welling replied, still fixing his attention on Peterson, sitting there looking as carefree as he did when he came in.

'And now?' Rosemount asked. Welling didn't look at her as he spoke, still fixated on Peterson.

'And now, Detective Rosemount I'm about to interview him, and I'll let you know what I think afterwards' Welling edged past them both and made the short walk down the corridor to the interview room.

Welling entered the room much to the clear delight of Phil Peterson.

'Good Lord, Mr. Welling, in all the excitement outside I didn't realize just how much you have aged in such a short space of time' Peterson said 'I thought I had been living a difficult couple of years'

Welling pulled out the chair opposite Peterson and sat down.

'Thank-you, Mr. Peterson but we're not here to discuss my appearance, we're here to discuss why you murdered the reporter and indeed how' Welling responded. Peterson still maintained the same annoyingly calm smile.

'I believe we've already established why I murdered the hack reporter,' Peterson responded.

'Hack Reporter, Mr. Peterson?' Welling replied, 'You're not a fan of Mr. Henderson's work I can see.'

'I'm not a fan of anything sloppy and without a good degree of thinking Mr. Welling' Peterson responded, finally losing his grin.

'So, how did you murder the 'hack' reporter Mr. Peterson?'

'I shot him, Mr. Welling, but then that was also in the press wasn't it, you need me to be a little more specific, in order to prove my liability do you not?' Peterson had an air of total confidence, and it was the same inherently arrogant attitude that had made Welling dislike and suspect him before.

'Then give me the specifics, Mr. Peterson, because we really have no time to waste,' Welling said.

'He's kidnapped again hasn't he?' Peterson said.

'Or perhaps he's told someone to kidnap again Mr. Peterson, because from what we've established so far, he doesn't do the kidnapping himself he gets others to do his dirty work for him, doesn't he?' Welling leaned forward to such an extent his nose was practically touching Phil Peterson's. 'Which begs the question, if he doesn't do his own dirty work, who took your family and why do they still have your daughter, allegedly?'

'Allegedly?' Peterson responded 'I can assure you I am not making that up, Mr. Welling'

'We will have to take your word for that, Mr. Peterson, because there's certainly nothing else to back the information at present' Welling replied, settling back in his chair 'Now, Mr. Peterson, give me the specifics, tell me something the public haven't already seen in the hackneyed press'

'Well, Mr. Welling, whilst I may have shot the reporter, I used a muscular relaxant, a paralyzing drug if you like, in order to prevent him from becoming too much of a handful' And there it was, the answer Welling and the Detectives had been waiting for, the only fact kept from the press. Peterson indeed appeared to be their man.

'And how would someone like yourself come across such a drug, Mr. Peterson?' Welling enquired, needing to know as the traces found in the toxicology report suggested Henderson had been poisoned with a substance unavailable on the common market.

'I made it, Mr. Welling. It's amazing how much you can learn from the internet isn't it?' Peterson said smiling again.

'Even so, Mr. Peterson, it strikes me as odd that you managed to get it so right, first time,' Welling said leaning forward again. For the first time since he'd entered the room Phil Peterson shifted uncomfortably in his chair.

'I didn't get it right the first time Mr. Welling. It took a few experiments before I knew what I was doing.'

Welling watched the expressionless smile reappear on Peterson's face.

'Experiment on what exactly?' Welling asked him, concerned with the possible answers.

'Some mice,' Peterson said before exploding into a fit of laughter.

Welling was disturbed by Peterson for many more reasons than he had been a couple of years ago at their first encounter.

'You seem completely and utterly unperturbed by the fact you have taken another life, Mr. Peterson. Irrespective of whether it was to save your daughter's, you seem totally oblivious to what you have done.' Welling's words stopped Peterson's laughter in its tracks and he leaned forward himself, his nose now millimeters away from Welling's.

'My daughter is worth more than some two bit reporter, Mr. Welling. We haven't lost a cure for cancer with the passing of Mr. Henderson. Nobody was crying in their morning cornflakes I can assure you.'

Tom Welling rose from his position. 'Thank-you, Mr. Peterson, I'm sure we'll speak again,' Welling said as he exited the room.

The two Detectives met Welling in the corridor and he beckoned them back to the viewing room.

The three of them looked at Peterson sitting alone in the room, still smiling to himself.

'He's your man,' Welling said, looking both Detectives in the eye.

'We know we heard him, so now what?' Rosemount said 'We charge him and he goes away for it, but it doesn't solve the problem that somebody is out there controlling this whole thing'

Welling looked back at Peterson sitting in the room, the smart, well groomed, immaculately dressed, slicked back haired man and spoke again.

'No, HE is your man he's the one. I've interviewed many murderers and a few serial killers as well and I can guarantee you this man is enjoying every minute of this. I know he killed his wife and daughter and I know he's responsible for doing this but we need to find out why. I need to get to Edgartown' Welling said.

'How can you be so sure though Tom?' Ashworth said, looking concerned 'what if you're wrong?'

'You called me here because you know I'm an expert Graham, not because I'm your friend and I am right that's your man right there and we need to work out why, to stop this. For all we know he could have set up many families with the same scenario' Welling paused 'Phil Peterson is here for a reason he came of his own accord, everything is being played out to his own plans, it must be, I can guarantee you he has thought this through to the letter. We need to move the goal posts and we need to change the rules, throw him a curve ball' Welling looked on at Peterson as he spoke. Watching the man sitting there, his gut told him they had 'Noah' they had 'The Choice Maker' right there, smiling alone in that room.

Detective Ashworth stormed out of the room and crashed back into the interview room.

'Philip Peterson I am charging you with the murder of Michael Henderson, reporter for the Massachusetts Times'

Peterson clasped his hands together and opened his mouth in mock surprise.

'Well Detective, I did do it after all,' Peterson grinned.

Chapter Fifteen

Mike Sanders banged and smashed his fists on the bedroom wall. 'What have you done with my Wife?!' he screamed at the top of his voice. 'let us out you son of a bitch' There was no response. The room he had woken in was immaculately decorated, well looked after and extremely tidy. Thick pieces of wood had been nailed to the inside of the windows to stop him looking out and people looking in. The curtains had been shut behind the wood, so from the outside it just appeared they were closed. All that featured in the room was a bed, anything that had once been there before most certainly had been removed in preparation for this. There were clear indentations in the carpet where furniture had recently been situated.

'Let me out' Sanders said again in a defeated, pleading tone, attempting again to kick in the heavy oak door. There was no chance, he was trapped.

Mike Sanders felt sick to his stomach. Whatever was going on, his wife was elsewhere and that worried him the most, he had no idea what had happened. One minute he was watching television and the next, awaking in this room. He felt as if he had been stuck here forever, but it was probably a lot less time than he realized. He'd taken his watch off and put it on the side when he returned from work and right now he was regretting that hugely. He went and sat on the bed and stared at the blank walls, noting the slight discoloration where photos had also recently been taken from the room. Whoever had done this was in no mood to be recognized he figured and wondered, not for the first time, if this was the home of someone he knew. Mike could hear seagulls in the distance and realized he was at least still near the sea. Having no idea how long he'd been out for it was difficult to say for sure, but Mike felt certain he was still in Martha's vineyard.

Meanwhile Gloria, Mike's wife, sat on the bed in a dingy basement. Her head still ached from the chloroform. She had a distinct memory of someone forcing himself into the house but then after that, a total blank. Gloria looked around the basement, it was untidy and stacked with boxes, as most basements generally were. A place to dump the unneeded crap you'd probably never intend to look at again anyway.

Apart from the bed, she was surrounded by a large amount of junk. She feared for Mike's safety, she wondered where he was and she worried that John had been taken as well. Had whoever done this just taken her, had they all been taken or God forbid, what if her son and husband were dead? It didn't bear thinking about but the thought couldn't help but replay itself over and over in her head, forcing her to relive the frightening possibility on a constant loop. Gloria knew the police had caught Barry Monkwood and she knew he'd committed suicide and yet she couldn't help but feel this was related in some way. Why shouldn't it be? Nothing ever happened in Edgartown anyway so what chance was there something terrible would happen consecutively but not be related? She was frightened.

The steps that led up and out of the basement were quite long and as she gazed up to the top she realized with horror, someone was sitting at the top of the steps, head in hands.

'Oh God, Mike is that you?' she whispered, her delicate tones still reverberating around the stony room.

The figure at the top of the steps raised its head from it' hands.

'No Ma'am' the voice of a man replied quietly and politely

'Who are you then, have you been brought here too?' Gloria asked, her voice audibly shaking with fear.

'I'm the one who brought you here Mrs. Sanders, I'm the one who took you and your husband' he said, sounding practically disgusted with his own words. 'It was me.'

'Why, WHY?' She shouted at him, frustration and fear pumping adrenaline around her veins.

'Because that's what I was asked to do,' the man replied.

'Where is my husband?' Gloria asked the man. He remained seated at the top of the steps and as she edged closer she realized he had covered his face with a balaclava.

123

'Your husband is elsewhere but he is safe I can assure you,' the man responded.

'I can't accept the assurance of someone, some animal, who had kidnapped us both. Have you hurt my son?' she screamed, wanting to know but dreading the answer.

'Your son isn't part of this, I haven't taken him, I did exactly as I was told to do.'

'You're ashamed of yourself that's why you've covered your face, you don't want me to see you' Gloria Sanders said, still petrified by the figure at the top of the steps but willing to show backbone anyway. The man rose from the steps and opened the door at the top to leave, as he did he glanced back down the stairs.

'No that's not it, I don't want you to recognize me' he said, before closing the door behind him and locking Mrs. Sanders back down below.

The weather was cool and yet Terrence Denton lay swathed in beads of sweat. His breathing echoed heavily around the room as the throws of deep sleep engulfed him. Denton had been plagued by visions since childhood and his affinity with the spectral being had made him infamous throughout Massachusetts and beyond.

Whilst Terrence was used to seeing and more often hearing the occasional echo of the departed on a daily basis, his knack for premonition was in its infant stages but had been growing rapidly. In the past six months alone Denton had seen, within his own dreams, various matters which had transpired to indeed happen.

Most recently he'd felt sure he had a fix on the missing woman and her child who had recently been found murdered and he was equally sure they were both alive when he'd envisioned them.

Now as sleep overthrew him again, Denton's dream felt as though it had paralleled itself with reality once more. His breathing grew shallow as the mind's eye replayed a movie through his sleeping but active brain.

There was a man and a woman, their faces as clear as day, he could detail every feature in them. He felt as though he was watching them unnoticed as Ebenezer Scrooge visited his former and future selves, like a ghost from Christmas present. The man and woman were sitting together talking, but he was unable to hear what they were discussing. Suddenly another man entered the room, but his face was shrouded in mystery. He was not wearing a mask but the mind's eye was unable to see exactly what he looked like. The man spoke however, and more became clear.

'If you agree to this I can let you go, that is all I have to do, nobody dies, nobody suffers,' the man spoke. Now Denton could hear the words of the woman sitting on the sofa.

'Apart from us,' she said.

'I'm sorry, I really am, but it's the only way,' the man spoke again. Suddenly the man seated with the woman on the sofa rose, and spoke himself.

'And if we say no you'll kill us?' he said, in a dejected non-aggressive matter of fact manner.

'The choice is yours, Mr. Sanders,' the man replied as Denton jumped awake.

'Jesus,' he said, grabbing the pad and pen he'd been keeping by the bed. Turning on the bedside lamp Denton frantically scribbled away, detailing as much of the dream as he could remember before it disappeared back into his sub consciousness. Denton was aware it may have been nothing more than your common dream but he'd been fast learning to take noting he saw in his sleep for granted.

Chapter Sixteen

Tom Welling disembarked the Chappaquiddick ferry, before being swiftly met by Chief Anthony Leith and his deputy Jenny Clearwater.

The chief drove him to the local town hall where they'd decided to hold most of the Edgartown investigation. It was a big old wooden building and it had a lot more space to move around in than the cramped stagnant office the two of them shared.

Anthony had set a white board up at the far end that suited Welling fine as he had plenty of notes to make.

'So no Detectives today then?' Anthony asked, pleased neither of them was there.

'Nope, you're stuck with me, they're working on the case in Boston. I'm going to fill you both in on the detail now and then we'll go from there' Anthony stopped to look around the hall, it smelt vaguely of old classrooms and momentarily took him back to childhood. Old desk wood filled his nostrils and the faint aroma of chalkboard dust invaded his memory, if nothing else. 'I like this room' he said.

Welling immediately made his way over to the white board.

'OK let's trace events, from the start to where we are now' He began jotting away on the board speaking to himself as much as the Chief and Jenny. The two police officers took purchase on some old chairs that had been stacked at the sides of the hall.

'Firstly we have the abduction of Claire and Jake Bradfield' he writes this on the board and then stands back and looks at it, as if he is teaching himself. 'Mr. Bradfield, the husband and Father, he gets 72 hours for no apparent reason to decide which of them will live and die' Welling writes this on the board before pausing again.

'He fails to make the impossible decision and they are both murdered, by it would seem Mr. Barry Monkwood, a local clown impersonator' jotting that down Welling begins to circle the board, walking behind it and then back to the front scratching his scalp as he does.

'OK and Mr. Monkwood, he tells us he abducted the two and murdered them because his own wife and daughter had been abducted themselves and that he was told to do it. Complex' Welling wrote this all on the board as point number 4 and then stepped back.

'But' he said scratching his chin 'Mr. Monkwood's wife and child were found murdered and buried in his garden, knowledge of which resulted in him killing himself, we think…' he stopped in mid-sentence 'or, we think he took his own life because the game was up…but no, that's not what happened, there's more here' Welling stopped again.

'Boston's foremost reporter meets you guys' welling turns and points at the two officers, acknowledging them for the first time since the three of them had entered the room 'and then gets murdered in a Boston hotel room' writing this on the white board Welling walks to the far end of the room and then back again. Anthony felt it was like watching a caged lion pacing up and down. Like the lion, there was more going on behind Welling's eyes than anyone could possibly imagine.

'In the meantime, another couple are abducted, WHY? Welling shouted this last word from the back of the room and then jogged back to the board, writing this down. 'Mr. and Mrs. Sanders, why you Mr. and Mrs. Sanders?' Welling asked a question nobody was about to answer.

'Then out of the blue we have a confession from Phil Peterson for the murder of Mickey Henderson' Welling stopped and turned around to face Anthony and Jenny again. 'Now you don't know Mr. Peterson but I do and as far as I am concerned, Peterson is the only constant here' Welling said, pointing at the board.

'How do you mean, the only constant?' Anthony asked.

'His wife and Daughter were kidnapped two years ago under similar circumstances. They were never found. He chose to save his Daughter, never got his Wife back. Now, out of the blue he claims his Daughter is still alive and he was told he would get her back if he killed the reporter' Welling stopped to jot more notes on the white board.

'What do you think?' Anthony asked Welling, his back still turned as he surveyed his list of scribbles on the white board.

'I think the whole thing is completely implausible starting with Peterson's original story about his wife and daughter. We missed something there. I think this man is behind everything that's happened thus far, but what is his motive?' Welling's question was rhetorical.

'But then who has Mr. and Mrs. Sanders if you have this man in custody?' Jenny asked.

'Good question' Welling said, pointing at her as he did 'A patsy, another stooge, someone else who, like Monkwood was in fact is, living under a threat from this man. It's a very clever game, literally getting everybody to do your dirty work for you, very clever indeed. What efforts have gone into finding the missing couple?' Welling said.

'We're looking but they could be anywhere' Anthony said.

'Indeed they could and everybody's a suspect, that's the intelligence of the crime' Welling said this with an air of respect in his voice. 'I think I'm going to need to go back to Florida and check out Peterson's domain there, something is unanswered and uncovered and the case could be solved right there' Welling looked back at the whiteboard and scanned his notes again. 'Handing himself in, taking ownership of Henderson's murder that's part of the plan. He wants to get close to the case, he's enjoying it'

Chapter Seventeen

Phil Peterson stood in the court in the clothes he had entered the police station in just a day before. Detectives Ashworth and Rosemount stood by as the Judge read out the charges.

'Do you have anything to say in your defence, Mr. Peterson' the Judge enquired.

'Only that you would do the same if it meant seeing your child again your Honor' Peterson said, quietly and respectfully. He was not the same condescending and arrogant Phil Peterson they'd had in the cell the previous day, however, both of the Detectives were already wary of this man and knew full well this could easily be a rouse and most likely was.

The Judge appeared to resonate with the comment somewhat, his eyes showing a smidge of sympathy as Peterson's words left his lips.

'Well I am very sorry, Mr. Peterson, whilst I do understand, and this case is transpiring to be one of the strangest I have ever come across, the fact remains, you have admitted to taking another life' the Judge replied. He paused and looked down at the Detectives 'I trust this man's circumstances and the commendable fact he has handed himself in to the Police, save wasting their time further will reflect when it comes to sentencing. You will have your day in court, Mr. Peterson, set for 10am, four weeks today' The judge paused again, seemingly mulling something over in his mind. He took a swig of water from the glass in front of him.

'You will remain in custody until this time, Mr. Peterson, however, I will set bail at one hundred and fifty thousand dollars'

'Your honor, with respect this man has pleaded guilty to Murder' Ashworth interrupted 'I don't believe bail should apply in this case'

'I do not take kindly to my authority being questioned in court Detective' the Judge replied 'Whilst I do understand your concerns the fact remains this man has handed himself in and in my personal opinion is not a danger to society and I am sure, if indeed he is able to afford bail, then he will remain in Boston, as are the conditions and attend trial as I expect him to'

Ashworth shook his head in disbelief whilst Rosemount remained stationary, eyes focused on Peterson. She was sure she picked up on a slight momentary smile on the corners of Peterson's mouth, but in a flash it was gone.

'There's a man here to see you' one of the desk clerks said as the Detectives made their way back into the station. 'He's sitting over there' he said pointing in the direction of Terrence Denton, the local psychic.

'I know that guy, thinks he's psychic, yeah OK throw him in my office' Ashworth said before he and Rosemount took Peterson back down to the cell.

'Well Peterson you're not coming up with the bail money anyway so you may as well enjoy your holiday for the next four weeks' Ashworth said, locking Phil Peterson back in the cell.

'Now, are you sure you want to represent yourself?' Rosemount asked him.

'Yep' Peterson responded, smiling 'Nobody can represent me better than I can'

Ashworth laughed 'Yeah you've done a sterling job so far Peterson'

Detectives Ashworth and Rosemount led Terrence Denton through to the interview room.

'I know you, seen you on the TV,' Rosemount said. 'I like your work.'

'Thanks,' Denton said as he took a seat. 'Unfortunately it's been with me from an early age so I thought I may as well use it.'

'Use it to make lots of money you mean, Mr. Denton?' Ashworth said.

'I'm offended Detective. I generally read for free, come and see my place, I'm not a rich man,' Denton replied.

'Why did you say 'unfortunately' Mr. Denton?' Rosemount enquired.

'Basically it's a gift that keeps on giving and by that I mean, I never have a let up, so unfortunately, I'm plagued with it if you like. So I may as well use it to help others,' Denton replied.

'Very noble of you' Ashworth said sarcastically. 'So what can we do for you today?'

Denton ignored the remark; he had grown used to such comments. 'I've been having visions of a man and woman, more than once now and I think they're in trouble. It's hard to say, but it's as though they have to make a decision, like that poor man whose family were killed,' Denton said.

Ashworth laughed and shook his head.

'We have enough on our plate at the moment, Mr. Denton, without interrogating your dreams as well,' Ashworth replied.

'I'll be back in a minute' Detective Rosemount said, before swiftly leaving the room.

'Listen I don't expect you to believe me Detective. I'm fully aware of how far out it sounds and if I hadn't been living with it for so long I'd be right on board with it alongside you, but I know what's a dream and what's a vision, this is not a dream I can assure you, it has meaning,' Denton said.

'Ok, ok let's say you're right, then where do we go, what are we meant to investigate?' Ashworth responded, 'We can't very well send a Detective for a walk around your mind'

'I know that but if anything I'm saying means something to your guys that can be of help then that's a good thing, right?' Denton answered as Rosemount came back in the room holding a photo. She placed the picture of the Sanders family on the desk in front of Denton without saying a thing.

'That's them, that's the couple in my vision,' Denton said, surprised.

'They've been abducted,' Rosemount said, 'We think the case is linked to the other one and probably to the death of the reporter Mr. Henderson,' she continued.

'Are they from Edgartown as well?' Denton asked.

'Yes, yes they are' Ashworth replied.

'I think I should go there, can you take me there?' Denton replied.

'No, I think he should come with me.' Nobody had seen Tom Welling enter the room and his voice took them all by surprise.

'And where are you going Tom?' Ashworth asked.

'Florida, I'm reopening the investigation into Peterson's family's disappearance. I think we solve that, we solve everything' Welling answered.

131

'And in the meantime Mr. and Mrs. Sanders wind up dead somewhere?' Rosemount said, looking angered with Welling.

'Well that's what you guys are here for, grill Peterson, talk to the Son, use the police over there in Edgartown and find them' Welling walked into the room as he spoke and shook Denton by the hand.

'I'm Tom Welling, I'm a criminologist' Welling said.

'I know who you are, I've read some of your material, it's very interesting' Denton said.

'You can't honestly think taking this nut job to Florida with his mumbo jumbo bullshit will help Tom?' Ashworth said, quickly following up with 'no offence intended' blurted in Denton's direction. 'Thank God for that' Denton said under his breath, prompting a wry smile from Rosemount.

'Do you fancy coming to Florida to work on this case?' Welling asked Denton, completely ignoring Ashworth's question.

'Definitely, I'd love to be of some help, but why Florida?' Denton asked.

'Long story, I'll fill you in on the flight' Welling replied.

'So you're going ahead with this then, you think the 'psychic' can solve the case?' Ashworth asked, his sarcastic wit becoming too much to bear.

'I firmly believe that thinking outside of the box can result in success so yeah, Mr. Denton could pick up on something missed before because God knows we definitely let things slip last time we were in Florida at Peterson's place, I'm certain' Welling replied.

'By we you mean you' Rosemount replied, looking Welling in the eye.

'Yes Detective Rosemount, I mean me. I've fucked up somewhere along the line and now this has spiraled out of control' Welling responded.

'You don't need to blame yourself Tom and anyway, you may be wrong about Peterson' Ashworth said.

'I'm not,' Welling replied. 'That's the only thing I'm one hundred percent certain of in this case, Peterson is the architect here and always has been.'

Chapter Eighteen

Peterson cut a lone, solitary figure, sitting upright on the bed in his holding cell. It had been the same cell only days before Barry Monkwood, the sad old clown, had hung himself from the sink. The irony was not lost on Phil Peterson.

The cold dank cell with its white walls and floor engulfed him as if a stone and tiled blanket.

Peterson wondered how his life had become this way and considered how things had been just two short years ago. Short years to most people that was but to him, the past two years had felt as though they were a lifetime. Peterson's life, his very existence, had changed beyond recognition in those two years. Everything he'd worked hard for, everything he'd aspired to be, gone in the blink of an eye. With nothing more than time to kill, Peterson's mind drifted and began to reminisce.

Phil Peterson's wife Barbara came through the front door carrying various bags of shopping.

'Hey let me get that honey' Phil said, grabbing the bags off her. They were heavy but Barbara had a strong arm, she was a well-respected netball coach at the local school and her athleticism regularly stunned even Phil, she was much fitter than him that was for sure. Barbara's tall, athletic build, flowing blonde hair and crisp as the ocean blue eyes made her a catch in any man's books but she belonged to only one man and that man was Phil. They'd met in a bar in town, clichéd as it seemed and had hit it if off immediately, that was eight years before. Now after seven years of marriage the two of them were as inseparable as ever.

Phil was an architect, a great one as well and Barbara didn't need to work, but wanted to. She loved teaching kids and she believed in the importance of educating them of their health and well-being at all times. Nowadays too many children spent their lives stationary in front of a video games console, their minds and bodies getting unfitter by the day.

Emily, the couple's six year old Daughter walked in the kitchen as Barbara began to unpack the shopping. She was the epitome of a mini Barbara, like a scaled down model. Her flowing blonde hair, however, had been restricted into plaits, mainly due to yet another outbreak of head lice in school.

'Look Mummy I made you this' Emily held out a concocted piece of art, paper stuck on paper, colors upon colors. Essentially it was a mish mash of a mess, however, it had been made for Barbara with love by her Daughter and that in itself made it a priceless work of art.

'Oh thank-you honey, it's gorgeous' Barbara said, without a hint of irony and with 100% honesty, it really was gorgeous as far as she was concerned.

'I know' Emily said matter of factly, before skipping out of the kitchen back to where she had come from.

Phil re-entered the kitchen. 'Eat out tonight?' he said.

'Fancy that?' Barbara answered.

'Yeah why not, we'll go into town with Emily, get a Chinese, you know how much she likes Chinese food. Are you up for that?' Phil said.

'More than, good idea' Barbara said before wrapping her arms around Phil's neck and planting a big wet kiss on his cheek.

'Ugghh that was a soggy one' he said laughing.

'You love a soggy one' she said, licking his face like a dog.

The three of them got ready and ventured on the short drive into town for a meal. Emily was over excited, she loved eating out and a Friday night meal out with mum and dad was always a good indication of the start of a good weekend, which might even result in a trip to the cinema at some point. She wasn't overly fussed with going to see a movie, not as much as she was with choosing popcorn, candy and a drink that was as big as her head.

Phil ordered the same things they usually did, lots of tit bits and finger food, something Emily loved. She was less into the sloppy, messy aspect of Chinese food, but she loved sesame prawn toast, a pancake roll and prawn crackers, they were her three favorites.

Their random dishes served, Barbara took the opportunity to make her way to the ladies room.

'Hey honey why don't you try and use the chopsticks today,' Phil said to Emily.

'Uhhh huhhh' Emily said shaking her head in disapproval at the suggestion. 'I like using my fingers'

'But it's exciting trying different things, go on have a go with the chopsticks, like this,' Phil said, picking them up and demonstrating how best to use the things, spilling rice and noodles in the process. Emily laughed and a little cheeky glint in her eye suggested she had thought of something. Suddenly picking up a chopstick Emily stabbed it right in the middle of some prawn toast and picked the whole triangular piece up with one stick, prompting Phil to roar with laughter.

'That'll do it I guess honey,' Phil said, still laughing. Phil's gaze was momentarily distracted by events at the far end of the bar, his wife appeared to be having a set to with a couple of guys propped up by stalls. As he left his seat to intervene, his wife returned, her face reddened and angry.

'What was that about?' Phil asked, distressed at Barbara's obvious upset.

'Nothing couple of drunks sitting at the bar, made lewd comments that was all, I was just telling them to grow up' She felt across her arm to her left breast.

'They touch you?' Phil said, still standing.

'Forget it Phil, it's nothing,' Barbara said. 'Come on, we'll go.'

'No, fuck that,' Phil answered, moving quickly down the restaurant to the small bar situated at the end.

Two overweight clichés wearing lumberjack shirts and stinking of beer sat at the bar laughing. Phil tapped one of them on the shoulder.

'Yeah, what do you want?' the guy said nonchalantly his idiot friend laughing still like a loon.

'I want you to apologize to my wife,' Phil said, gesturing to Barbara.

'That's your wife?' the guy responded, no longer laughing. 'Jesus mate, I am so sorry…I am so sorry you are punching way above your weight,' he laughed again, his friend following suit.

'You think you're funny guys yeah, picking on a family out enjoying a meal, you think you're clever yeah?' Phil said.

'Listen friend I was just pointing out that me and Matt here could show her a good time, and looking at you, I know we could. Why don't you let us boys take her home and teach her how to fuck properly for you.' The two goons started laughing again.

Phil pressed the tip of the chopstick he was holding to the man's throat.

'I think I can put this right through your fucking jugular, what do you think?' Phil said, looking the man in the eyes and smiling as he did.

'Go fuck yourself you prick,' the man said, no longer laughing.

Phil pulled away. 'You should really think about your actions guys, you never know what could happen in future,' Phil said, walking away. The two guys started laughing again. 'Freak' one of them said.

Emily sat quietly in the back of the car on the way home, trying not to listen to her mum and dad argue but it was unavoidable. The evening had been ruined.

'You shouldn't have said anything Phil, you should have just left it,' Barbara said. 'They were a couple of pissed up morons.'

'Yeah, well maybe so, sweetheart,' Phil responded sarcastically, 'but perhaps if you didn't walk around dressed like that all the time you wouldn't draw the attention.'

'Oh fuck you Phil, fuck you, maybe I should just wear a hijab if it keeps you happy,' Barbara screamed shrilly in retort.

The argument continued all the way home and until Emily was put to bed by her teary mum, who closely followed her by retiring to her own room. Phil remained downstairs, TV on but unwatched as he stewed in his mind over what had happened.

Looking at the clock Phil realized there was still twenty minutes until chucking out time. Those two disgusting pricks would be there until then he knew that for sure. He could make it back there before closing and really show them what he was made of. A more rational single minded person would have switched off the TV and made their way to bed but in a rage Phil was neither of those things and fifteen minutes later he found himself parked outside the Chinese restaurant, waiting.

Perhaps in the time it had taken him to drive to the Restaurant Peterson should have calmed down, taken stock of the situation and seen some reason. Unfortunately Phil Peterson, whilst mild mannered the majority of the time, had a tendency to lose his temper and struggle to find it again for some time. Many of the arguments he'd shared with Barbara were as a direct result of his hot headedness. For the past 6 months he had been visiting a therapist, attempting to assist him with his anger management issues. Sitting outside the Chinese restaurant hoping the two drunks were about to leave, it was clear the sessions hadn't been working.

Peterson sat silently, digging his fingernails into the steering wheel constantly, unaware he was even doing it.

A single droplet of water fell on the windscreen and ran like a lonely tear swiftly followed by a cascade of water as the heavens above opened. The warmth of the car, mixed with the colder air outside and the rain led to the windows on all sides of the vehicle rapidly steaming up. Peterson ran his hand over the inside of the driver's side window in order to clear his smoked vision and regain sight of the opening to the restaurant.

As he did, the door opened and the two drunks staggered out laughing into the rain, neither of them barely able to walk in a straight line.

Peterson's anger rose again, he felt the skin on his back tingle as the rage engulfed his whole body. It would have been all too easy to jump out of the car right there and go to work on those two imbeciles but even in his fit of rage, Peterson knew he should bide his time and wait for a secluded area. His right hand clasped the heavy hammer that lay on the passenger seat. Peterson intended to really give those two morons a good going over, a real fright. They would think twice before they ever lay their hands on another man's woman again and they would certainly think twice before opening their big, slovenly, drunken mouths.

Starting the engine so as to clear the windscreen with the fan, Peterson primed himself ready to follow the two staggering drunks for as long as he wanted, until the time was right.

Slowly creeping along for five minutes in the pouring rain, Peterson followed the two men. Their inebriation was such they remained completely oblivious to his presence throughout the entire time.

Eventually the two men stumbled down a dark, squalid looking alleyway. Peterson figured it could be a short cut as much as it could be a place for them to sleep. Given their current state either option was viable.

Peterson brought the car to a halt and parked at the side of the road adjacent to the alleyways entrance. Clutching the hammer he quietly left his car and stood in the rain. Hood of his dark coat up standing hunched in the downpour, clutching a hammer in his right hand Peterson looked as though he'd walked straight out of a horror slasher movie. Only this was completely real.

Apart from the sound of the rain hitting the cars and streets all that was audible to Peterson was the sound of laughter and stupidity coming from the two men up ahead in the alleyway.

Peterson walked on, entering the darkened narrow passageway and in the streetlight ahead could see the two men, only about thirty yards in front of him.

'Hey fuckers,' he shouted, prompting the two men to stop and turn in his direction.

'Who is that?' One of the men answered and then laughing 'Lenny, is that you?'

Peterson swiftly made his way forward, tightening his grip on the hammer.

Now facing the two drunks he reached up with his left hand and pulled down his hood.

'You never apologized' he said as both of the men stared at him. In tandem they both began laughing.

'You have to be fucking kidding me' one of the men said, leaning forward in fits of laughter. As he did he realized Peterson was holding something. What it was dawned on the man just as the hammer smashed across his cheekbone. The second blow hit him with such venom his left eye fully popped out of the socket, his face instantly a bloody mess. Seeing his friend, face smashed in with his eye dangling on his cheek, was clearly a sobering sight as the other drunk turned to run.

'Fuck,' he said, real panic in his voice, just as the hammer rained down on the back of his skull, claw end. A jet of blood flew in the air as the hammer met with scalp, skull and then brain in an instant. The formally laughing drunk goon was dead before his body hit the ground, copious amounts of blood running black in the rain soaked alleyway.

The other man was on his knees, barely conscious, but sobbing all the same.

'We're sorry, we're sorry' he gurgled through a blood filled mouth.

Peterson smiled at the man on his knees and looked down on him pitifully.

'Now don't you wish you'd said that earlier, your friend wouldn't be dead right now and you wouldn't be missing half your face,' Peterson said, still smiling. 'You know what though, you were an ugly fucker when I met you before, who'd have thought it possible you could look even uglier' As he finished his sentence he smashed the claw side of the hammer into the top of the man's skull, killing him instantly.

Peterson stepped back and surveyed the damage, his dry cold smile, never once leaving his face.

Making his way back to the car, hammer still in hand, rain continuing to wash down his face, Peterson embarked on the short journey home.

Barbara was asleep when he climbed into bed, seemingly unaware he had been out and equally unaware she was in bed with a murderer. Barbara's husband and Emily's father no longer existed. In an instant, Peterson had gone from being the normal hard working family man they knew and loved, to a cold and heartless killer. As much as Peterson would try and justify it to himself the fact remained, he had not been defending his wife's honor, he'd stroked his own ego with excessive force and released a side of himself which had been stifled, waiting to appear, for many years.

Welling and Denton sat in their seats as the plane sped down the runway, readying itself for takeoff.

'I'm not a fan of flying,' Welling said, as the plane left the tarmac and magically glided in the air.

'It's not flying you're afraid of,' Denton said.

'Oh really? You try sitting in my shoes then and see how you feel,' Welling said, his fingernails clasped firmly in the arm rests of the seats, as if that would somehow help if something did go wrong.

'No, there's not a person on this plane who's afraid of flying,' Denton said again, looking smug with himself.

The plane began to level out as it reached altitude and a number of people were clasping their nostrils tight and blowing through their nose to try and eradicate that feeling of deafness you often get on take off.

The passenger sitting in the seat ahead looked back at Denton and Welling. 'You're wrong there fella, I damn near shit my pants every time I come on one of these things,' he said to Denton, making Welling laugh out loud.

'Seriously guys, when you're on an airplane, it's not the flying you're afraid of, it's the falling,' Denton said, 'because when it's flying, you're all tickety boo, but when it's falling, then you'll be forgiven for shitting your pants.' Denton laughed as he said this.

'He has a point,' the man in front said, turning back round again.

'So you're more than OK with flying then?' Welling said.

'I should have been on American Airlines flight 11' Denton said.

'You've lost me,' Welling said. 'What do you mean?'

'I was booked on American Airlines Flight Number 11, from Logan Airport where we've just flown, on September 11th'

The man in front turned around again. 'Now this I am listening to,' he said. 'You're telling me you should have been on the first plane, the one which hit the North Tower?'

'Yes, yes I am,' Denton said, no longer smiling but quite solemn and sad.

'Oh fucking great, now we're on a plane with a Final Destination candidate,' the man said.

'Seriously, you should have been on that flight?' Welling asked, intrigued. 'Why wasn't you'?

'Fate and a little bit of supernatural intervention I'm sure,' Denton said.

'Oh here we go, this guy is some kind of wack job,' the man in front said.

'OK we don't mind you rudely listening to our conversation but can you turn round and keep your trap shut at least?' Welling said to the man.

'Couple of faggots,' the man replied, turning his fat neck back around.

Denton smiled at Welling and shook his head.

'OK so the morning of September 11th I'm booked on that flight, on my way to a conference in New York later that day,' Denton paused as if reminiscing. 'Strange day' he continued.

'You're not wrong strange day, worst thing I've ever seen,' Welling said.

'No I don't mean that, I mean yeah, yeah it was terrible but just a weird, fate enriched day,' Denton said. He went on to tell the story.

Denton was pretty anal, in fact borderline OCD, everything had to be checked, once, twice, thrice he had a real problem with accuracy. Not such a bad thing, it could be worse, but there were times when he just wished he'd trusted his own judgment the first time, rather than the fifth. The morning of September 11th had been odd from the off. The first thing Denton noticed was the complete absence of his paranormal 'friends'. For once he had woken completely alone, as if they were elsewhere. For most people the lack of ghosts in the house would be a Godsend, but for Denton it was an unnerving opposite. There was a certain comfort to having his faceless friends in tow at all times. As strange as it would seem to the layman, he felt alone without them and that morning was no exception. Denton explained that on the occasion when they weren't there he felt uneasy, as if they were gone forever. There was a perennial part of him that was forever concerned his gift would eradicate and disappear even though it was often more than a burden.

Fortunately the preoccupation of that mornings impending travel distracted Denton enough that he didn't really think too much about it.

He had an old sports hold all that he took pretty much everywhere and was the ongoing abode of his passport, forever zipped in the side pocket waiting for its next adventure. Lightly packing his bag for a singular round trip, coming back the same evening, Denton checked and re-checked his passport and tickets were there. Everything was as it should be. After five times of checking, Denton was convinced of it.

His preparation was complete and he was put into gear by the toot of the taxi cab's horn outside. Grabbing his hold all Denton made his way out to the cab and got inside.

After a couple of minutes the cab driver made the usual inane small talk but Denton was in no mood for chit chat, he just wanted to get to the airport and get on. To the dismay of his well preparedness the traffic was unbelievably awful, considering it was prior to rush hour.

'So where you off to?' the Cab driver asked in a tone heavily laden with accent.

'New York,' Denton replied, looking at his watch. 'If we ever get to the Airport,' he added.

'Ah don't worry, we always get you there on time,' the cab driver responded with a smile. 'New York, the place where dreams are made they tell me'

Denton laughed at this, he'd seen numerous dreams fail and falter in New York and not many made that was for sure.

'Where are you from?' he asked the Cab Driver, accepting as he was stuck in traffic he may just as well conduct some small talk with his current chauffer.

'Afghanistan,' the man replied, smiling 'I come to America to make my dream,' he continued.

'And do you like it here?' Denton asked him. The cab driver nodded his head in the affirmative. Nothing more was said for the rest of the journey. Denton sat there panicking he was going to miss his flight and the cab driver seemed to be contemplating other things, probably home, Denton surmised. After what seemed like an age the cab arrived outside the airport entrance and Denton swiftly made his way through the doors. There were literally minutes to spare.

Running over to check-in Denton unzipped his bag ready for his passport and tickets. Placing his hand inside all he could feel was the smooth cloth of the hold all and nothing else. He peered into the vacant pocket knowing it couldn't be so, nothing had been taken out. Denton's panic turned to relief when he realized it was the pocket on the adjacent end of the bag that he needed. Unzipping the opposite end the same feeling of dread was mirrored as previously but accentuated more so, this pocket was empty also. 'That can't be,' Denton said to himself. It was impossible, completely and totally impossible, but there it was, nothing in either end. Denton turned his bag inside out, neither the passport nor tickets were there. Between home and the airport they had gone. He momentarily accused the cab driver, perhaps he had taken them in some kind of identity theft. Denton put that thought to the back of his mind and was disgusted with his abject racism. Resigning himself to the fact he had missed his flight, Denton left the airport glancing briefly into the departure lounge as the people he was meant to share a flight with boarded. Only hours later Denton's envy of those people would turn to sorrow and despair.

As he finally arrived home Denton threw his bag to the floor and sat in the lounge, switching on the TV. Looking down at the bag he saw some paperwork, just poking out of one of the side zippers. Unzipping the metal teeth Denton saw, to his utter surprise and anger, the passports and tickets he'd been looking for all along, exactly where they should have been. His annoyance was short lived, as he watched smoke engulf the World Trade Centre. It wasn't until later that day did he realize he should have been part of it.

Welling sat, mouth agape, at the whole story. 'That's incredible' he said.

'I often wonder if the reason I woke up alone that day is they were pooling their own individual energy to make sure they helped me, because someone definitely watched over me that morning' Denton said. Neither Denton or Welling said anything for a few moments until the silence was broken by the man in front. He turned around to look at them both.

'What a crock of shit,' he said.

Chapter Nineteen

Mike Sanders sat silently on the bed in the walled in room. He'd exhausted all energies trying to make as much noise as possible and attempting to escape. He knew there was no chance of getting out of there and the fear of that realization sent a sickening lurch in his gullet. He couldn't begin to comprehend what was going on or why he was here. Worse still, he had no idea what had happened, if anything, to his family. Not only trapped in the room Mike Sanders was trapped with his thoughts constantly running away from him, creating scenarios of the worst kind in his head.

Sitting there silently Mike was startled by the door suddenly opening. There in the doorway stood a tall figure, clothed in black, his face disguised by a balaclava. Pointing a gun at Mike the figure spoke.

'Leave the room and slowly make your way down the stairs. Try anything silly and I will shoot you.'

The voice was less than menacing, practically pleading with Mike to just do as he was told. Mike did as was asked, slowly leaving the room and walking past the weapon clad figure and making his way down the stairs, the man close behind him.

'Do as you are told and this will all be over very soon,' the figure spoke.

Sanders crept down the stairs and into the adjacent living room. There sat Gloria, his wife, her hands and feet tied but she was alive. Relief met the panic in Mike's heart. Why was she here as well, what was going on? Seeing his wife bound on the sofa filled Mike with overwhelming rage, he turned swiftly taking the figure behind him on the stairs by surprise and knocked the gun out of his hand and over the banister, sending it clattering to the floor below.

'Wait,' the masked man said but it was too late. Mike smashed him as hard as he could in the stomach with his right fist and the masked figure doubled over, collapsing backwards on the stairs.

The commotion caused Gloria to look up and scream at the sight of her husband, grappling with this potential maniac on the stairs.

'Mike be careful' she cried in sheer panic.

Sanders grabbed the balaclava and peeled it from the man's face.

'Jesus' he said, taken aback, standing on the stairs to overlook the man 'I know you, I fucking know you' Mike said, still staring at the man in disbelief.

'You both do' the man said, sitting up 'this is not all that it seems, so please stop hitting me'

Gloria looked from her position in the living room and gasped herself.

'You're a police officer' she said, in stunned belief.

'I'm Officer Jed Dooley, of the Oaks Bluff Police Department' Jed replied.

'You have some explaining to do' Mike said, before making his way down the last few steps and picking up the gun. He felt the cold steel in his hand and proceeded to aim it directly as Jed.

'Wait' Gloria shouted 'He's the police.'

'And he kidnapped us, so what the fuck is going on?' Mike said, pointing the gun at Jed Dooley.

'Stop aiming that gun at me,' Jed shouted 'I'll explain everything, but you have to trust me'

'Trust you!' Mike said 'Trust YOU, I'm going to take a lot of convincing. Right now, all you need to do is convince me why I'm not going to shoot you with this' Mike said, waving the gun around in the air.

'And I will, but you need to hear me out,' Jed replied.

Mike beckoned with the gun and directed Jed to the living room.

'You can start by untying my wife and then we're both going to sit here and listen to everything you have to say and you better make it bloody convincing because there's little stopping me putting a hole in you right now' Mike said, beginning to sound power crazy with the weapon in his grasp.

Jed sat down and put his head in his hands.

'This has all got so out of control' he said, not making eye contact with Mr. and Mrs. Sanders. 'This is all I know, so bear with me and hear me out' Dooley continued, rummaging through paperwork to the left of him 'I got this' he said, handing a piece of paper to Mike Sanders. There were some hand written numbers on the top of the paper and a written instruction. 'Mr. Dooley, kidnap Mike and Gloria Sanders. You have 72 hours to make them transfer $200,000 into the above account number. If you fail, your parents die...involve your colleagues and EVERYBODY dies'

'How do we know you didn't write that?' Gloria said, her voice carrying an air of skepticism. Mike nodded his head in shared agreement.

'It's a fair point' Dooley replied, I guess I am asking you to take my word for it.

'Our son?' Mike asked.

'He's fine, he's over with the Edgartown PD as far as I am aware, he's in no danger' Dooley answered looking Mike Sanders in the eye 'As far as I can tell, the only way for everybody to get out of this is for that money to be transferred into that account'

'What makes anyone think we have that kind of money anyway?' Gloria asked. Mike smiled.

'I'm an investment banker dear, it's not too hard to hazard a guess' Mike replied 'And yes, I have that kind of money, Mr. Dooley, but I fail to see why I should abide by this piece of paper. You've already told me my Son is OK and irrespective of what this says, you're not going to kill us if I don't give you the money'

'You're mistaken' Dooley replied 'I've seen first hand what this maniac can do, I have to save my parents and the only way to do that, by all accounts, is for you to transfer that money into this account number.' Dooley reached down the side of the sofa and pulled out a pistol before Sanders could even react, firing the trigger at Mike Sanders, the bullet penetrating his shoulder, sending him crashing to the floor as he dropped the handgun before him. Gloria Sanders screamed, shielding her eyes with her hands. Dooley calmly picked up the handgun and lent over Mike Sanders lying on the floor.

'I'm Oak Bluffs number one marksman' he said 'and that is just a flesh wound. So in answer to your question, do as the note says, and

I won't shoot you anymore or are you really willing to sacrifice lives for money?'

'You're crazy,' Mike yelled in Dooley's face.

'I'm being driven crazy!' Dooley yelled back 'now do as the fucking note says and we can end this shit right now'

Phil Peterson remained in his cell, whiling away his time with more thoughts of the past. The night he'd murdered those two foul-mouthed thugs had been his epiphany. He realized he didn't have to put up with society's deadweight's if he didn't want to. Ever since that night he'd heard voices in his head, telling him what to do, all the time. The voice was his, an alter ego almost, continuously dictating how he should live and telling him who in his life he should fear. The fact he'd literally got away with murder had seemed to empower him even more. The act of murder hadn't disgusted him, the effect had been opposite and an incredible adrenalin rush but the knowledge that he had clearly got away with it, that had given Peterson an incredible sense of invincibility, he enjoyed that more than anything. Over the course of the next few months Peterson became distant to his wife Barbara and his Daughter Emily. He was increasingly more aggressive at work and had in some cases become practically unapproachable. If Barbara ever attempted to speak to him then he would snap, biting her head off with rhetoric of vile abuse. As if that wasn't enough he became more dependent on drinking, alcohol took him to a different place. Ultimately though, the one thing he needed, the one thing he desired the most was the bloodlust, that didn't seem to alleviate no matter what he did. Peterson had become a cliché, unable to satisfy any of his desires, unable to feel happy without firing into some kind of aggressive rage.

After another evening consisting of a speechless dinner with his wife, his eyes fixated on the television although never taking any of the pictures in. Peterson decided he needed something else to do.

'I'm going out' he said, rising from the table. Barbara didn't even answer, she didn't need to, she knew he had no desire to hear what she said anyway. It had been six months since Peterson had murdered the two men in cold blood and whilst Barbara had no idea he'd done this, she was markedly aware of the change in his personality in the last half a year. She had decided that he must be having an affair; such was his cold distantness towards her. Their relationship had always been strong but in such a short space of time, the distance between them was cavernous and worse still, Barbara felt as though she no longer really cared.

Peterson took the relatively short drive into town and made his way through the darker, poorly lit areas that most people would rather avoid than attend. He cruised around with no idea what he was looking for but acutely aware he needed to do something, anything, before he went home. He was craving some action. Up ahead Peterson saw a woman standing on one of the street corners, leaning up against a streetlight. Her miniscule skirt, knee high boots, revealing blouse and heavily made up face told him all he needed to know. She was a prostitute, a lady perennially of the night. He pulled the car over and wound the window down.

'Hey' he said 'get in' She didn't even ask him why, she knew, and she walked around to the passenger side and climbed in the car.

'I'm Amber' she said. He hadn't asked. 'Clive' he lied, as he pulled away from the curbside.

'So what do you want to do?' Amber asked, her lifeless eyes, devoid of all soul, long since screwed out of her, staring out of the windscreen.

'Do you have a pimp?' Peterson asked. Amber looked at him surprised 'Yeah, why, are you a cop?' she asked.

'No I fucking hate cops' Peterson said, partially telling the truth. 'I just wondered how much it would be to fuck you in front of your pimp, that's all' he continued, never once taking his eyes off the road.

'Nobody has ever asked to do that before' Amber said. 'I'm not sure he'd be up for that, he's my boyfriend'

'Really? Some boyfriend. Sends you out to do this, anything could happen to you and yet he won't watch another guy fuck you' Peterson said, finally looking over at her. She was a mess, she didn't look great under the street light but up close, a mess. Her skin was mottled and acne ridden and her teeth looked yellow and exceptionally unclean. She was unattractive and probably a drug addict to boot, Peterson thought to himself.

'You're very pretty' he blatantly lied.

'Thanks' Amber answered, not in the least bit interested 'Listen I'll phone my boyfriend and ask him, that OK?' she said. Peterson thought for a second.

'Yeah, no problem at all, I don't see why not, what's your cost anyway, for straight sex?'

'Oh fifty dollars' Amber replied. Peterson tapped his fingers on the steering wheel as if he were thinking.

'OK well tell your boyfriend I will give you one hundred and fifty dollars if I can fuck you in front of him'

She pulled out her mobile phone and called her pimp. Peterson was disgusted by prostitution but more disgusted by the people that ran it, the whole process sickened him. He knew this girl was almost certainly the victim of some street filth who had ruined her life to pay for his drug habit. It worried him that something like that could happen to his own daughter. It only took falling into the wrong crowd once and your life could be changed forever.

Amber put her phone back in the bag and zipped it up.

'Yeah he's up for that, it's fine, I'll show you the way' She proceeded to direct Peterson to a derelict, run down block of apartments deeply immersed inside the inner guts of town. The area brought new meaning to squalid and dingy, it was beyond awful. There were drug dealers, and crack whores all over the place. Peterson was immediately concerned about the safety of his car, not himself, but decided there was no option but to take a chance, his adrenalin was already pumping. For the first time that evening and in a long time, he was struck by a small amount of fear. It occurred to him that he was alone in the most run down part of town and outnumbered. Parking his car where he was told, Peterson followed Amber up a narrow set of stairs to a doorway on the second floor and waited as she let herself in. The apartment smelt terrible, a mixture of alcohol, excrement, urine and burning, it was disgustingly squalid. A tall heavyset black man stood in what could loosely be described as a lounge.

'Hey white boy' he said, smiling broadly 'You want me to watch you fuck my bitch?' he laughed heartily at this. Peterson disliked him instantly, he reminded him of the voodoo villain in Live and Let Die, his laugh echoing around the hollow apartment.

'Yeah I do and I'll give you one hundred and fifty dollars for it' Peterson answered steadily.

'OK White boy, you have a deal, you fuck her with your little white dick and then afterwards I'll fuck her properly' the pimp said, laughing again. Even Amber found this funny, or at least decided she should probably join in with the laughter to avoid a beating later. Peterson laughed too, the three of them standing there laughing together as the pimp berated and belittled Peterson.

'You're the big boss man yeah?' Peterson shouted, still laughing. Amber's pimp was unsure how to take this statement, he looked mildly puzzled, as if trying to establish whether Peterson was mocking him or being serious. It didn't take too much longer for him to realize it was the former as Peterson swiftly pulled out the gun he'd been hiding and pointed it directly at the pimp's head.

'Not fucking laughing now are you scumbag' Peterson said, looking sternly at the pimp.

'What the fuck are you doing white boy?' the pimp asked, before the bullet pierced his wind pipe, spewing blood everywhere in jets from his throat. Amber's abusive pimp fell to the floor as she screamed 'Brian' at the top of her voice in an agonized tone. He lay on the floor, his body jerking as he clutched at his neck, fighting to take some breath but it was too late, as blood pooled around his head and neck the life in his eyes faded and he was gone.

'Fuck Brian,' Peterson shouted at her, as tears rolled down Ambers face.

'You killed him, I loved him' she said through sobs.

'You loved him?' Peterson spewed at her 'You love a man that sends you out to make money for him selling yourself, you love that? You disgust me' Peterson said, enraged with her. He couldn't understand why this girl wouldn't be immediately overjoyed at the death of this piece of shit, lying on the floor in front of him. He felt angry and confused, he was suddenly overwhelmed with hatred for Amber and engulfed by her wailing sobs. In a moment of sheer blood boiling rage he shot her in the face, killing her instantly. The shrill sound of her cries immediately ceased by the boom of the gunshot and the slumping of her lifeless body to the ground. Peterson looked at the two bodies on the floor, knowing full well the Police would never care enough to investigate this fully. It was just more shit off the street for them. He felt fulfilled for the first time in months. For the first time since he killed those two men in that rain soaked alleyway. Peterson's heart pumped, his head felt woozy with joy, he was in his element.

He was taken back to the time he stole Mrs. Brody's cat when he was a child. He took hours torturing it before finally killing it slowly and dumping its limp, lifeless corpse in her garden. The adrenaline rush he got from hearing that silly old woman's screams was the same as this. Death was invigorating.

The cab Welling and Denton collected from the airport made its way through various areas of the state on route to Wellings home. They arrived in the vicinity shortly after five in the evening. It had been a good journey in and the weather was nice, not too hot, with a pleasant cool breeze. The sun was hanging dead center of the sky, bathing Key Largo in its golden rays. The cab pulled up outside Welling's beautiful Dolphin Avenue home and the two passengers disembarked.

'Nice place you have here' Denton said, removing his small hold all from the trunk of the car.

'Thanks' Welling answered 'Years of catching this great city's scumbags have helped pay for it'

'The least you deserve then' Denton quipped.

'You're not wrong either' Welling replied smiling. 'If it's OK with you, I'll introduce you to the family, we'll have a spot to eat and then we'll get ourselves over to Peterson's place and have a dig around'

'Sounds good to me' Denton replied as they embarked up to the front of the house. Making their way through the long entrance Denton admired the large number of framed family photos on practically every surface of the house. Welling was clearly a family man. A tall boy of about sixteen made his way down the stairs 'Hey Dad' he said to Welling.

'Sean this is Terrence Denton, a friend of mine, he's helping on a case' Welling said. 'Yo' was all Sean replied with, nodding in the direction of Denton. 'Where's your mum?' Welling enquired as Sean pointed towards one of the doors to the right.

Welling led Denton through to the dining area where Marie sat at the kitchen table, reading a Good Housekeeping magazine. Denton looked around. Clearly Welling's wife didn't need tips on how to keep a good house. Welling walked over to her and kissed her on the cheek, she jumped slightly startled.

'Sorry, I didn't hear you come in' she said, turning her head and kissing Welling on the lips.

'Oh hi' she said to Denton, spying him standing in the doorway.

'Hey' Denton said, making his way to the table and holding out his hand, which Marie took hold of and lightly shook.

'Honey this is Terrence Denton, he's helping me on a case, Terry this is my wife Marie' Welling said.

'Denton, Terrence Denton?' Marie repeated back 'You're the psychic' Denton nodded his head in acknowledgement.

'I've read you, seen you on TV as well' she continued.

'You see dead people?' Sean said, entering the room 'like the kid in Sixth Sense?' Denton laughed as Sean spoke.

'Kind of yes, believe it or not that film isn't as far off the wall as you might imagine' Denton said smiling.

'Listen I'm going to order Pizza, Terry and I have some work to do' Welling said interrupting. 'I'm sure Mr. Denton will enthrall you both with tales of ghosts and ghouls over dinner' Welling said chuckling to himself.

'Your husband is a near believer, Mrs. Welling' Denton said 'I don't think he is quite as skeptical as he wants us to think' he continued.

'Well let's just say I have an open mind' Welling responded 'I brought you along didn't I? That shows I have some faith in your abilities I think' Denton nodded his head in agreement. 'Yes I guess it does, I hope I don't let you down'

'I have no expectation to disappoint Terry' Welling said 'But if you can offer some insight, a different scope, then I'm all ears'

The pizza arrived and the Welling family, plus their new guest, sat around the dining room table to eat.

'So, I'm dying to know, how and when did you realize you have this so called sixth sense' Marie asked Denton, while pulling apart the crust of her slice of pizza. Denton sat there and relived the story of Davy Merrison, a story he'd told many times before and then shared the 9/11 tale again, a story Welling was pretty sure he would never get tired of hearing.

Eric Blane picked the half pound burger up from the wooden chopping board it had been served on. The excessive greasy residue that was left behind was enough to clog an artery on first sight. As he chomped down onto the saturated beast he broke wind, loudly. The rest of the people sitting in the fast food restaurant looked around at him. Eric Blane didn't acknowledge the noise, neither did he care, he just carried on chewing away, as comfortable as if he were sitting in his own front room.

The mobile phone he'd placed on the table in front of him began to ring, the familiar sound of the Muppets theme reverberating around the restaurant.

With his fat greasy fingers he picked up the phone and answered it with a food filled mouth.

'Hello' he muffled through a mixture of bun and beef.

'Eric, it's Anthony Leith, I was wondering if you could come over here' Antony said.

'I'm having lunch' Blane replied, taking another mouthful of saturated fat.

'It's ten thirty in the morning' Anthony replied.

'OK, I'm having elevenses then' Blane responded 'I'll be over soon, what's up?'

'I'm investigating the disappearance of Mr. and Mrs. Sanders' Anthony said.

'Oh, I thought those Boston Dicks were working on that, they don't want our assistance?' Blane replied, before he shoveled the last of his burger into his cavernous face hole.

'They can do what they wish, but I'm still the chief of Police down here and I'm starting my own investigation' Anthony responded with an air of determination in his voice 'You in?'

'Yeah why not, I'm bored down here now Dooley's on his holiday' Blane said, hanging up the phone on his last word. Gulping down the glass of coke he had Blane left the booth he was sitting in and walked out. A loud and violent burp left his lips just as he exited the restaurant drawing attention from most of the patrons and the giggles of a few of the children.

'Where are we going to start?' Clearwater said to Leith, as he dropped the phone in its cradle.

'I want to go back to the beginning, back to Barry Monkhood's house' he replied, picking up the pen from his desk and chewing on it.

'What do you expect to find there though?' Clearwater responded 'Ashworth and his team have already combed the place over'

'There's a reason Monkwood was chosen, something links him to that guy, Peterson, they have over there in Boston' Leith paused to chew on his pen again 'We're going to find it'

Chapter Twenty

Eric Blane arrived at Anthony Leiths small Edgartown office and walked straight in. The Chief and Officer Clearwater were already on their feet ready to leave.

'We're going over to Barry Monkwoods' Anthony said.

'He won't be there' Blane retorted laughing to himself. As usual, he was the only one.

With Leith and Blane in the front of the patrol car and Clearwater in the back they made their way over to Monkwoods house. When they arrived they could see the Police tape still cordoning off the entrance to the building. Taking out his pen knife, Leith sliced through the tape and then kicked the door open.

The house looked pretty much as it did the last time they'd been there, save for the forensics fingerprint dust all over the place.

'So, what are we looking for?' Blane asked.

'No idea, something that links Monkwood with Mr. and Mrs. Sanders, or the guy Peterson, the one who murdered the reporter or all of them even, who knows?' Anthony said 'Let's look through paperwork. Bills, letters, anything we can find, phone records, anything that may be relevant. If we go back to the beginning, we may just find the link that solves this case'

'This case is solved though' Blane said.

'It's not, we need the common denominator' Leith responded.

'We have that, he's banged up in Boston' Blane replied.

'I know that Eric but start thinking outside the box, what links that guy Peterson with Monkwood, with Sanders, with Edgartown?'

'Chief I think you're going to want to see this' Clearwater shouted from upstairs. Leith took the stairs two at a time, with Blane slowly trailing behind.

Clearwater stood at the landing looking up at the ceiling. 'Why is that opened?' She said, staring at the uncovered loft entrance.

'Can we do this' Denton asked nervously, as Welling jimmied open the back door.

'We can do what we like, we're trying to solve a case' Welling replied, smiling at the nervous tension on his new assistants face.

'What reason do we have to be here though, what will the police say if we get caught, it's burglary' Denton answered, sounding more like a frightened child than a grown man.

'For Christ sake Tom, I am the police' Welling said quietly, laughing under his breath.

'Yeah well why you whispering then?' Denton asked as the door clicked open, making him jump. This caused Welling to laugh again.

'And anyway' Denton whispered even more quietly, as if the door now being open was the signal to be even more careful 'you're a Criminologist, you're not the Police at all' Welling patted Denton on the back. 'Very good point, very well made' he retorted, sliding back the patio door and walking into the darkened room.

'What if someone is here?' Denton cautiously remarked, remaining outside of the doors still, not quite breaking and entering just yet.

'I doubt it, the owner is holed up in a cell in Boston and we're pretty sure his wife and kid are elsewhere, if not dead' Welling said, flicking on his flashlight. 'Now stop pussying around and come in, I need your expertise, see what you can feel'

'My so called expertise rarely comes to the party when I'm a nervous bloody wreck' Denton said, finally making his way inside, shakily like a lamb taking its first steps.

'What do we expect to find here though, really?' Denton asked 'haven't you looked before?'

'Not really, not properly' Welling said 'I always had a bad feeling about the guy but he was never a suspect and the Detective working the case, he never felt for one minute Peterson was involved, he felt sorry for him'

'So why did you feel differently, what made him seem so suspicious to you, why the doubt? Denton responded.

'We'll call it a hunch I guess, something never sat right with me about that guy and I've been proven right haven't I?' Welling replied.

156

'How?' Denton couldn't see the point of Wellings remark.

'Well he killed that reporter didn't he?' Denton said, 'The man is a murderer'

'I know that, but he was doing it to get kid back' Denton answered.

'Don't believe all you are told ' Welling said 'He handed himself in. He's been playing a game with us, not just since he arrived in Boston, from the start, since his wife disappeared all that time ago'

'How do you intend to prove that now?' Denton enquired.

'We're going to search this house from top to bottom, we're going to find something, anything, to link him to their disappearance'

'And what if we do Tom, then what does that prove, how does that link him to those deaths in Edgartown, what's the point?'

'Oh there's always a point Terry, always and we're going to find out what it is'

Officer Dooley sat facing John and Gloria Sanders, the butt of the gun clasped tightly in his hands.

'You didn't need to shoot him,' Gloria said, bandaging the bloodied wound on her husband's shoulder. Beads of sweat ran down his forehead, and dripped off the end of his nose. 'I told you, it's just a flesh wound' Dooley said.

'It feels more than a fucking flesh wound' John snarled at Dooley.

Officer Dooley didn't care anymore; he just wanted this over and his parents back. He was thirsty and so tired. He didn't want to get a drink because he didn't want to lose sight of Sanders for a minute.

'If you had just done as I asked this wouldn't have happened, you could be on your way now' Dooley said, looking at John.

'So we transfer the money and we can go, that's it' Gloria asked.

'Yes, well no not straight away, as soon as my parents are returned, I let you go, I'll get a call to say they're on their way' Dooley responded.

'Where the fuck does it say that on that piece of paper?' John shouted, practically spitting the words at Dooley.

'It doesn't' Dooley shouted back 'I had a phone call giving me instructions, you'll have to take my word for it'

'Yeah take your word for it' John replied 'Take the word of a corrupt cop who's abducted us and shot me in the shoulder, excuse me while I try not to laugh'

Dooley got out of his seat and pressed the barrel of the gun to John's forehead. Gloria screamed 'No, please don't!!' and started crying again.

Dooley pulled the gun away. 'I'm sorry' he snapped, not sounding sorry at all 'Do you think I want to be in this situation as well, do you think I want to be doing this?'

Nobody said anything, the three of them sat there in silence for what seemed an eternity. Dooley no longer knew what to do to encourage Sanders to transfer the money. He'd already shot him, which if anything had made Sanders even less likely to do as he asked.

'You're the Police for fuck sake you can get my money back, surely, after it's transferred. I mean, banks, banks can do anything nowadays, everything is traceable, we'll get the money back' John said, reasoning with himself if nobody else.

'Yeah, yeah definitely' Dooley said, not at all convinced or concerned at whether that were true or not. He had a glimmer of hope and he was going to take it. 'We'll get the money back, at most it's a loan, a loan to get us all out of this situation. See it as that, nothing more' Dooley was practically pleading with Sanders.

'Whatever happens John, it's only money' Gloria said 'You have a lot more than four hundred thousand in your savings John, much much more'

'Please' Dooley begged 'We're running out of time'

'He doesn't want a lawyer to represent him?' Rosemount said, her voice tinted with cynicism.

'Nope, wants to represent himself' Ashworth responded. 'As far as I'm concerned, that's great news hopefully his arrogance will dig an even greater hole and he's never going to be able to afford the bail set, so he's stuck here'

'What if he does though, what if the Judge lets him out?' Rosemount responded.

'Listen, you're worrying about nothing, he doesn't have that type of money and if he does, he could have declared it yesterday'

Ashworth answered 'Anyway, even if he ever was released on bail, we'd track him, keep an eye on him. Don't forget Rosemount, he handed himself in to us, this guy may be many things in Welling's opinion, but he sure as hell isn't a runner'

'Yeah I know, he doesn't seem like a runner, but Welling is certain he is playing a game with us' Rosemount replied.

'I trust welling one hundred percent' Ashworth said 'But he has a history with this guy and perhaps his view is a little clouded'

The two detectives walked down to Peterson's cell. As usual he was sitting there quietly, reflectively thinking. The click of the cell lock startled him and he looked at the door as it opened.

'Good Morning Detectives, I've been waiting for you' Peterson said, smiling.

'Waiting for what?' Ashworth said, not really caring to make small talk with the defendant today.

'Has there been any news on my Daughter Detectives?'

'If you mean, have we found where you buried her yet, then no Peterson, there hasn't been' Ashworth said.

'You're a very dislikeable man Detective Ashworth' Peterson replied.

'Very rich coming from a murderer' Ashworth responded.

'I'm feeling a little stifled in here, a little bored, I'd like to pay my bail bond and get out' Peterson spoke without blinking, smiling his usual off putting grin 'if I'm going away for a long time, I may as well spend as much time outside as I can'

'Is this a joke Peterson?' Ashworth responded, but felt uneasy by the sudden game change.

'I don't joke Detective' Peterson replied 'Now, let's get this sorted'

Ashworth stormed out of the cell, swiftly followed by Rosemount. Peterson watched the door slam behind them and continued to smile to himself.

'I'll miss our banter Detectives' he called after them sarcastically.

Peterson sat alone, neither pondering whether he could afford the bail bond or thinking about his future, Peterson had no real interest in either, he knew exactly what was about to happen to him. His eyes staring at the wall Peterson glazed over, disappearing back into his minds eye, watching the past unfurl before him.

Peterson sat at his kitchen table, the sun shone and it was a glorious Saturday morning, eating cereal drinking coffee and reading the newspaper. Turning to page 15 he spied a story he'd been expecting to see for a few days. A prostitute and a 'gentleman' had been found murdered. There were no leads. 'Gentleman' indeed Peterson thought. The guy had been a disgusting pimp scumbag and got what he deserved. Peterson figured the prostitute, she didn't deserve it but at the end of the day she was only going to have a life of crime anyway. He rocked on the kitchen chair, back and forth, preaching the moralistic to himself. That's right he'd done the world a favor, he should be awarded for his services to the public. Peterson knew full well there never would be any leads because the Police weren't interested. He felt safe, untouchable and invincible.

Closing the newspaper he decided to venture upstairs and see what Barbara was doing. She was completely unaware as he walked into the bedroom, tapping away on her computer obliviously. Peterson watched her as she typed, she was on some social networking site and chatting to some guy. He could make out the words 'Be good to see you too' as she typed. Peterson felt his blood boil as the hair on the back of his neck stood up with a cold chill. He couldn't see the man's face properly but he could see it was certainly a man from the profile picture. 'Who the fuck is she chatting to?' Peterson thought to himself, jealous rage encompassing him. He slowly and quietly backed out of the doorway so Barbara was unable to see him and gently made his way down the stairs again. Peterson sank down on the sofa, images of his wife rolling around with a faceless stranger etched in his mind. Oblivious to the fact his Daughter had wandered into the room, Peterson stared through Emily as she stood in front of him.

'Daddy' she said. He didn't answer, he was elsewhere in his mind. At that moment Barbara happily bounced down the stairs.

'I'm going into town to get some shopping honey,' she said, grabbing her coat.

Peterson snapped out of his daze. 'Take Emily with you,' he replied in monotone.

'Oh OK, what's up?' Barbara asked, sensing another mood unfurling. Phil's sporadic mood swings had made him practically unapproachable at times lately. Barbara had been worried about him but whenever she tried to broach the subject, he'd fly off the handle. He never wanted to talk anymore.

'I have a headache, I want to have a lie down in peace,' Peterson responded coldly.

Barbara didn't answer him, she could tell where this would head if she tried to respond or make any remote suggestion of conversation.

Barbara helped her daughter get her shoes and coat on and the two of them made their way out of the house. 'Bye daddy,' Emily said, but Peterson didn't reply.

No sooner had the sound of the family car engine drifted off down the road, Peterson had flown up the stairs to the bedroom.

Sitting at Barbara's computer he logged on. He didn't need to know her password because she didn't have one. Being irrational Peterson decided the reason she didn't have a password was due to the fact she DID have something to hide. In his off kilt world people with things to hide try their hardest not to hide them. Clicking on the saved favorites link took Peterson straight to her home page. She hadn't logged off, and now he was in. He could look at her friends, her statuses and more importantly, her messages. Now he could find out what she was up to and who was trying to take her away from him. At the end of the day, that was all that really mattered to Peterson, it was not that he loved his wife or cared for his family anymore. He hated the thought of somebody else having something that he considered his, something that he owned.

Chapter Twenty One

The gaping black opening of the loft looked down upon Leith, Clearwater and Blane.

'Could have been left open by Forensics the last time they were here?' Blane reasoned. It was a more than fair point. Leith considered the last time they'd made their way into a loft, at the Bradfield's place.

'Jesus Christ I'm gonna have to go up, but you're right, it's probably nothing'

Ever since he'd found the mutilated bodies of Claire Bradfield and her son, that image had been the last thing Leith had seen every night he closed his eyes for sleep. In truth, he hadn't really been sleeping at all since the case started, far too much on his mind. Only days before the Chief had been concerning himself with the futile nature of his position and now all hell had broken loose. In fact hell was alive and well, in his quiet little town.

Leith knew what had to be done and knew he was the one who had to do it. He reached up and pulled the ladder down. Nobody breathed, the only sound any of them could hear was the creaking of the loft ladder as it made its way down on the runners.

Blane reached over and flicked a light switch on the wall, causing a bright glow to emit from above.

'There's nobody up there' Blane suddenly broke the silence.

'What makes you so sure?' Clearwater responded, looking up into the well lit loft space, with the rest of them. 'Because we have our guy already, he's locked up over there in Boston' Blane responded.

'They think that's the guy' Leith answered, still looking above him 'they don't know it's the guy though'

'They've got the right one, I'm sure of it' Blane said.

'So who's abducted the Sanders then?' Clearwater answered. Nobody replied, they all just continued to look above them.

'OK, cover me' Leith said, gingerly taking one step at a time on the ladder, his gun out of the holster and held above his head. Entering above, from below, was never especially safe. Whatever they taught you in respect of covering yourself never amounted to much when it came to approaching danger above you. Leith was all too aware of that fact at this point, as his exposed head neared the opening.

Poking his cranium into the loft, Leith looked around, at first seeing nothing, just your standard room filled with a lifetime of junk. In the most undignified manner he clambered in on all fours, finally standing. 'Looks OK' the chief shouted down to the officers below, 'nothing going on here' as he made his way across the dust covered wooden floor, looking at all the boxes something lightly brushed the top of his head. Leith raised his hand as if to rub away a stray cobweb, but his hand hit something solid. Leith looked above him and made a loud yelp as he did, not through pain and not a scream, but through shock and sheer fright.

Above his head Leith saw two, not one, lifeless, limp corpses, dangling directly above him, looking down on him with dead, sunken eyes. Their grey pallid skin was broken only in color by the noose around their necks.

'Jesus Christ, for the love of God, we have bodies, we have bodies!' Leith screamed. Clearwater raced up the steps and was first to see the two corpses hanging from the rafters.

She put her hand over her mouth, stifling the desire to scream and vomit at the same time. Blane came up as quickly as he could. He set sight on the two nameless victims and sunk to his knees. 'Oh my Christ' he said, his head beaded in sweat 'it's Jed Dooley's parents'

Leith ran past Clearwater and Blane and bolted down the steps. Not stopping he made his way downstairs and out the front door, before vomiting on the porch. Once he had finished the Chief composed himself and wiped his mouth on the back of his hand, breathing heavily, before removing the phone from his inside pocket.

'Detective Ashworth, it's the Chief over at Edgartown, we have a situation here, a serious fucking situation'

'I love how modern technology can store all of our information, don't you?' Welling said to Denton, as he tapped his gloved fingers on Peterson keyboard.

Denton didn't say anything, instead he sat silently on the king size bed staring at the magenta coloured bedroom wall.

'Hey, you OK?' Welling asked him, not turning to look, still concentrating on the computer screen in front of him.

Denton didn't answer so at last, met by the stony silence, Welling craned his neck around. Watching Denton sit so quietly Welling hesitated to speak but then stopped himself, realizing Denton was elsewhere. Perhaps Denton had drifted to one of his far off places that could help solve the case. It was after all the reason Welling had brought him along in the first place. Revisiting his efforts on the screen in front of him, Welling continued to click away. The 'favorites' section on the computer veered without doubt towards this terminal belonging to Barbara Peterson. There were cookery sites, holiday sites, patterning sites for the purpose of decorating and one social networking site. Knowing Peterson, there was not a chance in hell he was signed up to anything like this. When Barbara had initially gone missing the Police had searched all of the obvious clues, her computer being one of them. Nothing had transpired but now, that was about to change.

Entering the site Welling was struck by a clear anomaly, hitting him like a brick straight between the eyes. According to the information in front of him, Barbara Peterson had last logged on just three weeks ago.

'Jesus she could still be alive,' Welling said loudly, as much verifying the information to himself as to Denton.

'I can tell you she's not,' Denton finally spoke.

'Well she's been on here,' Welling replied, gesticulating towards the computer screen.

'Somebody has I'm sure, but not her,' Denton replied, his voice level, almost cold and distant. 'She's here, she's here now and she has her daughter with her,' Denton said, his pitch never once changing.

The skeptic in Welling wanted to shake Denton by the throat and tell him to stop talking nonsense. However, there was a much larger segment of Welling's being that totally trusted Denton and believed him whole heartedly.

'They met an awful, terribly frightening end at the hands of the one person who was meant to protect them,' Denton said, his voice cracking as his sentence trailed off.

'You're sure?' Welling responded quietly.

'So sure, I can take you to their bodies,' Denton answered, finally looking at Welling.

'So who has been on here then?' Welling asked, looking back at the screen. Suddenly the realization of the situation dawned on Welling.

'She was friends with Barry Monkwood. Shit, look!' Welling said, startled by the information before him. Denton came over and looked at the screen.

It wasn't long before the two of them had gone through the list of Barbara Peterson's friends. Not only was she associated with Monkwood, she was connected to James Bradfield as well.

Welling then began opening message after message, all innocuous and friendly, to Barry Monkwood and James Bradfield. Within minutes Barbara Peterson's history was pieced together. Having entered the house a couple of hours before with a boxed jigsaw in his head, Tom Welling was pieces away from completing the puzzle.

'You've told me a fair few stories since we met Terry,' Welling said. 'Now I'm going to tell you Barbara Peterson's or at least what I think it is. I'll tell you something else as well, I'm very rarely wrong,' Welling confidently said. Denton wanted to know what had brought this innocent woman and her daughter to such a brutal conclusion in their existence. 'I need to know,' Denton said.

'Well from looking at this, Barbara Peterson had been raised in Edgartown as Barbara Fitzpatrick' Welling began 'She'd been friends with Barry Monkwood, James Bradfield and probably a great many of the other townsfolk over there. As people do she'd moved on, set up life elsewhere and started again. Often the case with networking sites she had caught up with friends of old, faces from her past. Nothing wrong in that but then something changed' Welling stopped and started at the screen again, his brain practically ticking in time with the clock on the wall, thinking. 'Her husband saw she'd been chatting to various guys on here I think, men from her past and in a jealous rage murdered his wife and daughter' Welling leaned forward in the chair 'Only you didn't then kill yourself did you, you coward' he was talking out loud to an absent Phil Peterson 'no, you decided to hunt down the men you thought were responsible for your rage, deflected the blame elsewhere didn't you Peterson, because that's what you do isn't it?' Welling leaned back in the chair and clicked on the messages again.

'Apparently Terry, Barbara Peterson was only chatting to Barry Monkwood again a few weeks ago, oh and did I mention she arranged to meet him?' Welling smiled 'Only you didn't meet him did you, you lured him away so you could take his wife and daughter and there your game played itself out' Welling left the chair and began to pace around the room. 'You have to hand it to him, it's quite clever really, two birds with one stone, gets the revenge he thought he was owed on Monkwood and Bradfield with one hit' Welling looked at Denton 'Which raises the question, why the Sanders afterwards?' Denton shrugged his shoulders 'She'd been chatting to him as well?'

Welling shook his head and muttered a puzzled moan 'No, she's not linked with any of the Sanders family on there at all, unless...' Welling stopped mid-sentence and ran back to the computer.

'Peterson wasn't smart enough to remove information from the computer what's the betting his history is still on here as well?' Welling replaced talking with more clicking of the mouse before he paused on a specific page.

'And there we go, only two weeks ago, the Boston rich list. Tucked away in the lower echelons is a Mr. John Sanders, Investment banker.' Welling smiled almost victorious. 'To the naked eye, his name doesn't even stand out as important, but still one of the richest people in Edgartown.'

'That doesn't explain why he'd be interested in him, look at this place, Peterson has money' Denton said.

'That may be so, but does he have enough to pay his bail money when he's on a murder charge? Almost certainly not' Welling said.

'Why did he murder the reporter?' Denton asked Welling, hoping for an answer.

'That was the smartest move of all, every good psycho wants to be part of the chaos they've created' Welling said with a touch of

166

admiration 'He made himself the center of attention without making himself a direct suspect for everything else that was going on. Ensuring the Sanders disappeared while he was already in custody, that was the icing on the cake and the one missing link we need, in order to find them'

'We need to get back to Boston then' Denton said.

'Absolutely but first of all I need to call Ashworth and tell him what we've discovered' Welling said, removing the phone from his pocket. In all the commotion and excitement of unfolding the case Welling hadn't heard his phone signal the arrival of a text message and a pivotal message at that. Wellings jovial almost childlike excitement at getting to the bottom of Peterson dissolved almost as quickly as the color did from his face. Looking at Denton, Welling spoke almost as distantly as his compatriot had earlier.

'He made bail.'

Ashworth looked at his phone as the call disconnected before glancing at Rosemount.

'He's guilty as sin' he said 'we've just dropped a fucking maniac to his freedom'

'What the hell are you talking about?' Rosemount replied.

'We need to get back over the Acorn Hotel right now and re-arrest Peterson, I'll explain on the way' Ashworth walked passed Rosemount as he spoke.

'We can't, he made bail' Rosemount shouted after him as he raced towards the stations exit.

'He made everything happen as well' Ashworth shouted back 'You're either coming with me Rosemount or staying here, either way, I'm gone'

Rosemount raced after him and made it outside just as the sound of the car engine exploded in the air. Ashworth revved furiously as Rosemount clambered in the passenger seat.

He explained all Welling had told him in the short time it took the two of them to drive the five miles to the Acorn Hotel.

The hotel was a quaint, three storied little place just on the outskirts of town. The Judge had ordered Peterson to stay in town and he had duly obliged. As courteous as he'd been since he handed himself Peterson had given the Judge no reason not to trust him.

After all, Peterson was as much a victim in this crime as anybody else, at least that is how he'd wanted everybody to see it.

Now Ashworth and Rosemount were aware of the facts they approached the hotel with caution and trepidation. If Wellings theories were correct, then Peterson was potentially lethal.

Only an hour previously the two Detectives had left Peterson in room 315, under the strict orders of remaining there. He'd been nothing but agreeable, seemingly happy just to be out of the cell. Peterson had even gone to the lengths of asking Rosemount if she could find anything out about his missing wife and daughter.

'You stay at the end of the corridor' Ashworth ordered Rosemount 'if he tries anything funny, gets by me, makes a run for it, he's only got one way to go, towards you and you take him down'

'We left him here on good terms, he may not even suspect anything' Rosemount said optimistically.

'It's possible he's manipulated this whole situation to the end goal of getting away, we have to be prepared for him to take flight' Ashworth said, frustrated by Rosemount's lack of foresight 'just wait here and watch' he said, practically exasperated.

Ashworth slowly made his way down the long corridor before finding himself standing outside room 315. He looked back at Rosemount and nodded before knocking loudly on the door.

'Mr. Peterson, it's Detective Ashworth, can I have a quick word please' Ashworth spoke loudly through the door. There was no sign of the door being opened and not the slightest indication of movement beyond it.

'Mr. Peterson, it's Detective Ashworth, are you OK in there?' he spoke louder still, banging his fist again on the painted ply wood. Still not a single sound emanated other than the rat a tat of Ashworth's knuckles on the door.

Rosemount stood nervously at the end of the corridor. Her air of optimism had been replaced by the distinct feeling of impending doom and fear. The lack of response from 315 had left her heart pounding in time with every thud of Ashworths on the door, she could hear her own heartbeat reverberating through her eardrums as her adrenalin began to rush.

Ashworth raised his fist again ready to thump the door one final time before he forced his own entry. He looked back at Rosemount just in time to see Peterson standing behind her, the gun in his hand aimed squarely at her oblivious head.

Peterson smiled at Ashworth, silently raising his index finger to his lips, menacingly telling Ashworth to be quiet.

'Cherry!' Ashworth shouted, as Peterson pulled the trigger, splattering the contents of Rosemounts head over the cheap flock wall paper of the hotel. Her instantly lifeless body fell to the corridor floor, all the living that remained spilling out and soaking into the carpet beneath her. Peterson disappeared from view as Ashworth tried to compose himself.

The undesired choice of fight or flight had taken hold and Ashworth was determined to battle and defeat this monster. He ran down the corridor, briefly glancing at Rosemount's body on the floor, trying hard to block from his thoughts what had just happened. Rounding the corner Peterson had just escaped down Ashworth was met with a teeth shattering fist to the jaw, his head dazed and ringing instantly. Dropping his gun as he fell, Ashworth fell back, hitting his head on the corridor wall as he did, the blurred vision of Peterson towering over him. He hadn't looked that tall cramped in the cell but now it was as though a giant towered over Ashworth. Landing in close proximity to his partner's body the Detective lay prostrate on the floor.

'Did they teach you nothing?' Peterson snarled at Ashworth 'this isn't the movies, I wasn't about to let you take chase for a few scenes, no, I just waited for you to do the obvious Detective Ashworth and my, you didn't disappoint did you?' Peterson knelt down and picked up Ashworth's gun. 'Now I have two, it's turning into a collection' Peterson said. Ashworth's senses were returning and the ringing in his ears subsided. The pain in his cheek was intense, the inside of his mouth on fire. From the taste in his mouth and the soft contours which his tongue found, it was clear he'd lost some teeth. It was also clear from the solid object jutting in his back, he had landed squarely on Rosemount's dismembered firearm.

'Get up' Peterson said, flicking his gun at Ashworth to signify he needed to rise. Ashworth deliberately rolled onto his front, maintaining the façade that he was disorientated and needed to push himself up on all fours. Discreetly clutching the barrel of the gun Ashworth managed to tuck it into the waste of his trousers as he rose.

He felt the end of Peterson's gun press against the back of his head as he stood.

'It's OK Detective Ashworth, I assure you I'm not about to give you the same grizzly end as Detective Rosemount' Peterson spoke the words in his usual cold matter of fact manner. When they'd had him in custody, his persona was gentlemanly but in it's current context, was nothing short of psychotic.

'Now Detective Ashworth, I want you to walk away from me, back towards the hotel room until I tell you to stop' Peterson remained calm and icy cold 'Do as I say and you won't die, now walk slowly please, very slowly'

Ashworth decided to do as he was told and wait for the opportunity to reveal his retribution for Peterson.

His expression without change, Peterson looked down at Rosemount's body as Detective Ashworth slowly walked away from him.

'It's a shame, it really is' Peterson spoke 'Detective Rosemount seemed very nice, she probably had a bright future. She still would have if you hadn't decided to come back here. I knew you would though, too much has gone to plan so far, something had to derail slightly' Peterson continued as Ashworth ground his teeth together, his body overtaken with rage.

'Ironic really as you Detective Ashworth, you I found quite detestable, it should be you laying here really shouldn't it' Peterson suddenly went quiet and Ashworth considered the possibility he had finally made his escape. Looking back over his shoulder Ashworth spied Peterson still standing there, the gun pointed in his direction as before.

'Nobody told you to turn around did they Detective Ashworth?' Peterson said smiling. Ashworth turned back and continued his long, slow walk back down the corridor.

'Yes, I liked Detective Rosemount' Peterson said, before Ashworth was knocked to the ground by a sharp, agonizingly painful jolt to the back matched with a loud explosion echoing around his head. Searing white hot pain burned down Ashworth's spine as the realization he'd been shot numbed only his brain. Ashworth knew the gun was there in his waistband somewhere and the desire to grab it and defend himself was outweighed by the pain that now engulfed the end of every nerve in his body. Peterson stood over Ashworth now, the ends of his shoes inches from Ashworth's face.

'It's OK Detective Ashworth, it really is, I'm not going to kill you and would you like to know why?' Peterson knelt down his warm breath rippling off Ashworth's ear. 'Because Detective Ashworth, you liked her even more and living with that will kill you a whole lot slower and much more painfully' Ashworth could hear Peterson's footsteps rasping in the carpet as he walked away, the last thing he did hear, before he eventually passed out.

Chief Anthony Leiths patrol car screeched to a halt outside Officer Dooley's house. Kicking the door open Leith raced from the vehicle to the front porch, not waiting for either of his passengers as he kicked the front of the house in.

Jed Dooley threw his hands above his head in surrender. 'Don't shoot!' he screamed. Anthony quickly spotted Mr. and Mrs. Sanders, sitting together on the other chair.

'Please I just need the call and they can go,' Dooley pleaded with Leith. The Chief immediately realized what Dooley was waiting for, news of his parents safety. The pieces of the puzzle began to knit together in his mind. Dooley clearly hadn't washed or shaved for a few days and looked not like a man on the edge, but a man long over it.

'Just let me take them to the car Jed,' Leith said. 'Nothing is going to change if I do.'

'You don't know, he could be watching, you don't know that' Dooley begged manically.

'Officer Dooley, I'm taking Mr.& Mrs. Sanders with me' Leith spoke slowly 'The man responsible for all of this is in Boston, they have him over there. I'll send Eric in to explain'

Leith nodded towards Mr.& Mrs. Sanders. 'Come with me please' He led the two of them out of the house and towards the car, Blane and Clearwater standing outside.

'How is he?' Clearwater asked. Anthony didn't answer, choosing instead to turn his attention to Blane.

'Eric I haven't told him, you're his senior officer, I think you should' Leith said. Blane nodded in agreement before patting Leith on the shoulder and making his way into the house.

'Is our son OK?' Mrs. Sanders asked with a worried crack in the tone of her voice.

'He's fine, there was never any danger to him' Leith replied.

'Oh thank God' Mrs. Sanders said, flooding with tears of relief.

'And our money, how will we get our money back?' Mr. Sanders said.

Chief Anthony Leith closed the car door and drove away, in time not to hear the anguished scream of 'Nooooo' erupting from Officer Jed Dooley's home.

Epilogue

Three Months Later

Tom Welling disembarked the Chappaquiddick ferry to be met by Anthony Leith just as he had the first time he arrived in Edgartown.

They shook hands and exchanged the usual pleasantries before Anthony drove the two of them to the town in relative silence.

Entering the Edgartown coffee house they ordered a drink and took their seats.

'So I read the bodies of Mrs. Peterson and her Daughter were recovered at last' the Chief said.

'Yeah, Denton was right, took us straight to the spot' Welling replied 'You know that guy is quite remarkable, he's going to be moving to Florida and working with me in future, he's ability is invaluable in solving cases' Welling paused as the waitress delivered their coffees. He nodded his thanks and took a sip. 'I wish we'd had him available sooner' Welling said.

Anthony nodded in agreement. 'Me too, we were all sorry to hear about Detective Rosemount'

'Terrible' Welling replied 'She didn't stand a chance'

'How's Ashworth doing now?' Leith asked, taking a mouthful of his latte.

'I've just come from there, he's a broken man' Welling replied 'He'll never walk again, he's going to be confined to a wheelchair for the rest of his life. They've said they'll give him a desk job but it's not the same and it's not him' Welling ran the tip of his finger around the rim of the mug.

'Dooley's the same, in pieces, I can't see him returning to work' Leith responded 'If it wasn't for Clearwater taking care of him, God knows what he might have done'

'Peterson certainly made sure he did a job on everybody he came into contact with' Welling said. 'Evil man' Leith replied.

'Clever sociopath' Welling responded 'As much as I hate saying it, he played his game well'

'Isn't hard when you're the only one who knows the rules' Anthony said 'You're no closer to catching him then?' he enquired, knowing full well the case had gone cold a month back.

'No I'm off it now, back home, just hope he slips up wherever it is he slunk off to with Sanders money'

'I hear Sanders is trying to sue the police force over that,' Leith said.

Welling laughed 'I know, the gall of the guy, he should think himself lucky he wasn't killed as well'

'This town is going to take a long time to get over what's happened here' Anthony said, gazing out the window at the quiet sunlit streets outside.

'it's like a shark attack' Welling responded 'As much as you don't want to be, you become forever associated with it. The pain will dim though, it always does'

Leith nodded his head in agreement as he took a final mouthful of his coffee.

'I guess I better be getting back' Welling said, extending his hand to shake.

'You didn't have to come all this way for a five minute chat' Leith said. 'We could have done this on the phone'

'True, but I thought it would be good to draw a line under the case, from your point of view at least and say our farewells' Welling said 'and anyway, I like this little town'

'Despite everything that's happened here since you arrived?' Leith asked puzzled.

'See, I guess the memory of the shark attack is wearing off already' Welling said 'I have a feeling Edgartown is stronger than that'

'Well either way I'll take you back, the next Ferry will be along soon' Leith replied.

Leaving Welling at the dock the two officers shook hands and went their separate ways. They'd developed a mutual respect for each other and promised to keep in touch and the Chief was sure they would.

Anthony Leith tooted his horn as he drove away, waving out of the driver's window as he did.

Welling stood at the water's edge, the ferry around 5 minutes away but in his line of sight. He sighed and then breathed in a huge gulp of Edgartown sea air. Wellings moment of meditation was interrupted by the vibration of his mobile phone in the inside pocket. The display screen flashed with the words 'Unknown Caller' as Welling answered.

'Hello, Tom Welling speaking' he said.

'Why hello Tom, long time no speak' Peterson's sickening tones reverberated in Wellings ear.

'How did you get this number?' Welling asked, startled by the sound of Petersons voice on his phone.

'You can get anything nearly you want nowadays Tom, you know that,' Peterson said.

'They'll get you Peterson, they always do in the end, we found you out once before we'll get you again' Welling said, anger rising in his voice as the thought of all those ruined lives flashed through his brain.

'Oh I don't doubt they will but be fair Tom, they couldn't even get me when I handed myself in' Peterson said, laughing 'and I shan't be doing that again Tom, no siree'

'Your confidence will ultimately be your downfall, it always is with people like you' Welling snarled.

'People like me?' Peterson asked 'You mean people like us, because you and I are very similar Tom, perseverance is the key and we always get what we want in the end don't we?'

'Well we can't both get what we want Peterson because what I want is to see you in the electric chair' Welling shouted the last words and the nearby seagulls flew off with a resounding squawk.

'Tut tut Tom, you can't let your emotions get the better of you' Peterson said 'and how is Edgartown?'

'How would you know I'm in Edgartown?' Welling said, startled by the question.

'Those gulls I just heard, call it a hunch,' Peterson said 'it's a lovely town, I quite enjoyed my time there' Petersons overbearing arrogance incensed welling.

'We found the bodies of your wife and daughter in the woodland where you left them,' Welling replied. 'Very noble of you shooting them both in the back of the head.' He said these last words with pure vitriol, he wanted to shame Peterson if that was at all possible.

There was no response from Wellings tormentor, but he could still here him breathing. Finally, after what seemed like an age, Peterson spoke.

'I have to go Tom, I'm a very busy man but before I do, would you afford me the opportunity to ask you one simple question?' Peterson said.

'Why should I?' Welling asked. 'How about I just cut you off now?'

'Oh don't do that,' Peterson quickly interrupted, you'd regret it I am sure, who knows when we'll next get a chance to chat? One simple question Tom?'

'OK,' Welling agreed, hoping it could be enough to trip Peterson up and reveal something, anything about his whereabouts.

'That's very kind of you Tom, really it is,' Peterson said without a single air of sarcasm. 'OK, here goes one question Tom.' Peterson paused, as if for dramatic effect.

'If you had say 72 hours from now, who would you choose to save, your wife or your son?'

The End

17175393R00104

Printed in Poland
by Amazon Fulfillment
Poland Sp. z o.o., Wrocław